BEING BLACK *in* VIETNAM

BEING BLACK *in* VIETNAM

Donald Talbert

Copyright © 2014 by Donald Talbert.

| ISBN: | Softcover | 978-1-4931-4473-0 |
| | eBook | 978-1-4931-4474-7 |

All rights reserved. No part of this book may be reproduced or transmitted in any form or by any means, electronic or mechanical, including photocopying, recording, or by any information storage and retrieval system, without permission in writing from the copyright owner.

This book was printed in the United States of America.

Rev. date: 02/06/2014

To order additional copies of this book, contact:
Xlibris LLC
1-888-795-4274
www.Xlibris.com
Orders@Xlibris.com
551863

Chapter I

You could really tell that summer was on its way out. A light mist that left a light fog all over downtown Flint, Michigan climaxed the cool brisk autumn air. There we were on this early September day, waiting for the busses to take us to the induction center in Detroit. Most of the Blacks all knew each other because we all lived in two areas in Flint, Michigan due to discrimination. On the North side of Flint we were in an area around Buick Motor Division with none of us living West of Saginaw Street or East of the Flint river. On the South side of Flint, Blacks were mostly congregated in an area called the Black Bottom, which was located on the East side of Saginaw Street. Grand Traverse on the West side and Thread Creek on the North, boxed in this area. Thirteenth Street bound the area on the West side all the way to Thread Creek. We also lived in an area called Elm Park located South East of Saginaw St. and extending from Court Street on the North side to Thread Creek on the Southside. I along with Raymond Vaughn were the most vocal of the group.

With less than ten minutes before departure time most of the busses were already filled when I finally showed up. A couple of the brothers with cars had taken up three parking spaces so all I had to do when I got there was drive up and park, right in front of the federal building. Once I got out of the car and walked over to where the crowd was, all the brothers began sharing stories about what they had taken to fail the physical.

Raymond and myself shared two slabs of greasy, salty spare ribs, which he had gotten from his fathers rib house. In the middle of our group conversation, we could hear the bus driver hollering for us to board the buses. As usual, all the brothers migrated to the same bus.

The busses were boarded and there was a brief wait before we were on our way. No sooner than we left the city limits everyone began listening to the portable radios that some of the fellows had brought along. The bus driver however, wasted no time complaining about the music. Raymond and I were seated in the front row right by the door and all the way down to Detroit we had to listen to his complaining.

The brothers in the middle and rear of the bus waited until we were on the road outside of Flint and began passing the booze and joints that had been brought along. The driver tried unsuccessfully several time to make them stop enjoying themselves, but no one listened. After the two-hour ride to the induction center at Fort Wayne in Detroit, the driver reported us and we had to stay on the bus while the other buses were unloaded and the future recruits were taken in to begin their physicals.

When we were finally allowed to leave the bus, we had to listen to the ridicule from the army personnel especially when we began to start our tests. The sergeant that was leading us through the different test areas would walk up to the testers and tell them that we were all trouble makers and they would run us through the different test at an extremely fast rate. One of the fellows questioned the tester about how his blood pressure was taken and he was told that, "You don't half to worry about it where you're going, Hot and Dry."

I remember the Army personnel asking about if any of us belonged to any subversive groups, only male surviving son, drug addiction, flat feet or bad backs. However, they didn't care, everyone in our group passed except Raymond and he had two doctors excuses. I mean they didn't care if you belonged to a hundred subversive groups, had a hundred dollar a day habit or if your arches had fallen completely out of your shoes, they were going to take us! We really became mad when we found out that the other busses had a forty percent failure rate.

In what seemed like only a few days we were back at the Induction Center taking our oath. To our surprise we were headed to Fort Polk, Louisiana instead of Fort Knox, Kentucky where inductees from Flint usually went.

The plane ride to Alexandria, Louisiana wasn't to bad but when we got there it was a different story. There was an army sergeant at the airport that welcomed us into the army and then we had what seemed like an all night ride on some rough riding army buses to Fort Polk. The next morning after we arrived we were sworn in and issued our clothing. During our ceremony they told us to raise our right hands to take the oath. Some of the fellows never even raised their hand and to my surprise the army personnel just smiled and kept right on with the oath.

I almost got kicked out the first day I had my uniform on when this young "Kid" sergeant was walking down the wooded walkway and headed towards myself and a couple of brothers. This youngster was coming up on the same side as myself, then all of a sudden he said, "Hey boy (talking to me, who was on the same side of the walk as he was) move out the way." The two brothers walking with me had to restrain me from jumping on him. I didn't care how many times he had been to Vietnam; I still didn't like what he called me.

As soon as I was assigned to a company this young kid came over to my company and told the drill sergeants (DS's) what had happened and that was the beginning of my troubles. The first day we were doing physical therapy (PT), I was in fairly good shape so I was keeping up adequately when one of the troops stopped doing the push ups and one of the DS's walked over to the trooper and kicked him in his butt. I really got mad and told the DS that I didn't play that shit and I asked the trooper why he let him get away with kicking him?

From that day forward, every chance the DS's got they would punish the troops and blame it on me. After a while my name became part of the training manual. Thank goodness for my demeanor from the streets because I was ready to fight at the first sign of trouble! The DS would always begin every exercise by telling the troops that if they kept up with him we could knock off early before we started our classes, but he already knew that I was usually the first one to stop and he took advantage of that fact. I can still remember him hollering at me to keep going! At first the other troops would be hollering at me to keep going and sure enough I would stop. Then the DS would stop and let one of the other DS's take over for our punishment, for me stopping.

When we first started going to the rifle range, they herded us into these five-ton trucks and away we would go. I remember the first day we rode out to the range I kept thinking of how long a ride it was. The next morning the DS's were all mad at me as usual and they made us put on our full combat gear, we even had our rifles.

After the morning formation they told us that the other DS had gone to the motor pool to get the trucks and we could wait for him. I should have known something was wrong when he was gone over a half hour.

Finally the DS came back and told us that the trucks were gone when he arrived so we had to start walking toward the rifle range. Our DS also told us that he would be on the lookout for the trucks while we were walking. My feet were hurting after we walked less than a half mile. I kept noticing that the closer we got to the gate, the faster we were walking. Then as soon as we got out the gate the DS's told us that there was a change in the schedule and the brisk walk turned into a fast jog. We had to be at the rifle range in less than an hour and away we went.

After the first ten strides I found myself out of breath and I was already looking for my second wind. I kept up for about the first fifteen minutes and then I slowly began to fade. The DS's saw that I was fading and they told the troops that if everyone made it to the rifle range they would assure us of a bus ride back.

You can just about imagine how far the rifle range was from the post (5 miles). One of the troops took my rifle and another grabbed hold of my arm and away we went. With the troops help, I made it another twenty minutes until we approached a long section of road that was filled with rocks and that really discouraged me from running any further.

So just before we got to the rocky part of the road, I fell down right on the shoulder of the road. The DS's came back to where I was lying down and were hollering at me to get up. They kept hollering until the bulk of the troops reached the rocky section and they made the troops low-crawled in the rocky section until I finally got up.

The troops were all hollering at me to get up, but they crawled about thirty feet before I finally got up and started to run again. All the troops were mad at me for making them crawl. Then four or five collapses later we finally made it to the rifle range.

After that incident, whenever we had a formation for work details I was somehow always chosen for one of the details. I caught pure hell all the time I was in basic training. When I was in the hospital for two weeks and on light duty for a week, I missed a lot of training and that didn't stop me from passing basic training.

The DI's told me that rather than put up with me for another six months they would make sure I passed Basic. When it came time for me to take the tests I had planned to put forth a good effort but not pass the tests. It was really scandalous the way I did on the written portion of the test. I would sit there a while daydreaming and then all of a sudden I would scratch a bunch of answers and then wait on the tester to call time. When I grew tired of daydreaming I would read the question and mark the wrong answers.

The pattern worked fairly well because I did manage to land in artillery instead of the infantry. I found out later that your score was how they decided where to place you in the different parts of the army and the better your score the better your options. I was really sick when I thought that I could have had some technical job that couldn't be done out in the field. The other end is that I could have ended up in the infantry, pounding down millions of miles of turf, dodging mosquitoes, mines, sniper bullets and snakes.

When the Physical Torture (PT) part of the testing came I managed to finish the first ten tests but not within the allotted time. Then came the mile run. The DS's had been building up the mile run all day, they kept telling us they wanted us to beat the other company's time because they had won the last four times. Also if we ran the best time the DS's promised to buy us three kegs of beer. The DS's knew all the time that I wasn't going to act right and they took advantage of the fact.

Right after lunch the DS's marched us back over to the athletic field for our final physical test the mile run. I remember as I was walking down the road headed towards the athletic field there were only a few people on the field as we approached the track. When we finally arrived I noticed that the few people there were the DS's that had left the mess hall earlier than us. The next thing I noticed was all the DS's had stop watches and not even the first sergeant was out there to witness the event. I knew right then that we weren't going to get any kegs of beer.

When I first walked onto the field and before I could prepare myself mentally the DS's were in a circle all around me telling me that if I do a good job they would forget all our differences. Everyone kept saying (even the troops) that they knew I could do it. The DS's said, "If not for us," well, for the troops. The DS's were really playing on my sympathy. After the pep talk the DS's had us all warm up (jumping in place) and stretch before we began our final event. Before long the DS's were asking us all to line up and start the mile run. As the race began I headed straight for the front of the pack. I figured that I really had the DS's now because I almost walked the last two hundred feet of the race. If you could only have seen the race. I started out leading the pack and after the first lap; there I was still holding the lead. The DS's were yelling and screaming at the troops to go faster. The DS's were also rooting for me because they were glad to see me, of all people, in the lead.

As we crossed the half-mile mark I had faded to fourth. That brought the DS's out to the edge of the track. The DS's were all screaming at me not to slow down any more, but by the time I had reached the three-quarter mark, I was struggling to hold 20th place. The rest of the way I would walk a while, jog a while and then fall down. I was trying to make sure that I didn't come any where close to the allotted time to finish the race.

I really thought I had the DS's and I was waiting for them to tell me that I had to take basic over again. However, that was until the DS's called me over by the finish line to tell me that since I had done such a good job of trying they would give me the same time as the last man to qualify.

I complained about not passing the test but it didn't do any good. The first sergeant said, "I will look into the matter with one breath and gave me my orders with the next breath." It wasn't hard to tell that the army personnel were just putting up with us because they already knew we were headed to Vietnam. I remember my last day in Fort Polk I walked around to some of the company's where the troops were taking Advanced Infantry Training (AIT) and none of the companies I visited had less than a half Black population.

After basic, I went to AIT in Fort Sill Oklahoma and things were going along smoothly for me until we went to this propaganda class. The instructors showed us some movies on what life was like in the Soviet Union. You know people forced to stand in the bread lines because of no food to speak of, people living in run down overcrowded houses. These houses were in such bad condition, where you couldn't leave the room while the food cooled off, once you cooked. The rodents wouldn't leave anything on the plates; this along with people lacking civil rights. Now this sounded like a legacy of Black America. Everyone knows just how we have been treated in this country.

The more I watched the movie the madder I got. Then after the movie came to an end the instructor got up and began telling us about how good we had it in this country. Just like the Black folks didn't exist. Once his pep talk ended the instructor asked if there were any questions about the movie or about communism?

A lot of hand came up because no one knew that much about communism, including myself. After the instructor answered a few questions, he finally called on me. I said, "From what I've seen in the movie and how they run things around here, well I can't tell the difference." Instantly the place sounded like a college basketball game after a slam-dunk because all the troops were hollering and chanting Yeah, Yeah, Yeah . . . The instructor was really mad at me and he had trouble trying to quiet the troops because no one stopped hollering right away. Not to mention the really dirty look the instructor gave me. I was close to the door when the class ended, so after class I took off before he could fish his way thru the crowd and stop me. Just about the time I got back to the barracks, the word had already come down for me to go see the captain. Everyone was saying the captain was going to kick me out of the army for saying what I did.

I waited until after lunch before I went to see the captain and he was really mad at me. I began telling the captain about how the establishment treated Black folks in this country and that I didn't say anything about how the army was run, but this was how Black soldiers are treated around here and once they leave the post. The next thing that I knew the captain was telling me to get back to my barracks and he would be keeping an eye on me.

Chapter II

When I first got to Oakland I was undecided as to whether I really wanted to go to Vietnam. I figured that I would look around the post first and ask a few people about what my chances of staying alive if I actually went over to Vietnam. Once I started to walk around the post I stopped this Black E7 and asked him how were they treating Black soldiers over in Vietnam? He told me to just do like I'm told when I get over there and don't make any waves. I should have known not to ask him, especially after I saw all those medals and ribbons he had plastered all over his jacket.

The second brother I talked with, I made sure that he didn't have a lot of medals and ribbons all plastered across his chest. He told me that he didn't have it that bad where he was, but you still could tell that things were not like they're suppose to be.

The first few days in Oakland, we were busy going to more classes about Vietnam and getting processed to go over seas. Then, once we were processed and the classes were finished we were told that we couldn't leave the post. I became angry and decided to leave the post and head back to Michigan, no matter what the consequences. The next day we were finally given our orders to leave after lunch and I decided to walk off the post and head for the bus station.

Around a half hour later I finally made it to the bus station. To my surprise I wasn't the only one who had decided not to go to Vietnam. There we were all six of us, two White, one Mexican and the rest of us were Black. Once we found out that the next bus heading north was seven hours away, we all headed to the bar.

It took us about five rounds before we decided to go back and stick it out. As soon as we left the bus station we caught a ride back to the base and picked up our gear. When we arrived at the air terminal the army folks had already been calling our names. We didn't even miss our flight, because to our surprise the plane was still being loaded and we continued walking until we reached the loading platform. The troops all gave us a standing ovation when we got on the plane because they thought we had all went home. I can still remember the sergeant giving us hell about not being on time.

Chapter III

Eight to ten hours later we reached Hawaii, about one third of the way to Vietnam and I was already tired of flying. Our second stop was Guam. Everyone was glad once we landed in Guam because we knew our next stop was Vietnam. As the plane left Guam everyone was in good spirits and you could barely hear the plane engines because of all the racket the soldiers were making.

After a few games of cards I dozed off like everyone else and we all slept until some engine noise woke us up. Some of the soldiers began making jokes about us being under fire. A few laughs later, we began to feel the temperature change. Then all of a sudden a voice came over the speaker, "Good evening this is the captain speaking, we are now entering the territorial waters of the Republic of Vietnam and we will be landing shortly."

When the captain finished no one said a word until the stewardess asked everyone to please fasten your seat belts and we will be descending shortly to begin landing. The temperature was getting hotter by the minute, a lot hotter that in Guam. When the plane finally came to a halt and the plane door first opened, the odor almost knocked me out, not to mention the sound of the shells being fired all around us. I knew right then that I had made a mistake coming over here.

As we approached the terminal at Thon se Nutt we could see all the troops that were waiting to go home. Some of the troops were happy and some sad. I began to wonder what I had gotten myself into?

As the last of us piled into the terminal some of the other troops gave us a standing ovation because they knew it was their time to go home. After the noise from the troops died down, I walked over and asked one of the brothers standing behind the roped in area, how he had been treated over here and he said, "About the same as they treat us at home." I really became mad and I made up my mind that I wasn't about to take any shit from these White folks.

Just to make sure I asked a few more brothers how had they been treated and they said about the same as the first one whom I had asked. The stories ranged from a Black who was wounded and sent to the hospital in country and then back to his company, while his white counterpart, wounded less severely was sent home to heal his wounds.

Another brother told me that his friend was wounded and was MISTAKENLY put with the dead bodies. Once his wounds healed he was sent back to his company and when he couldn't readjust, he was sent home with a 212 discharge.

After we left the makeshift airport, we traveled in a bus convoy to 90th replacement; where we were supposed to find out where we were going to be stationed. We arrived late at night and were herded into this area, liken to a sardine can, to sleep. The bunks were so close together that if you stretched yours arms you might hit someone in the mouth. We had to sleep on our personal possessions to keep them from being stolen, as a matter of fact; most of the troops with us took turns sleeping to make sure their belongings weren't stolen.

You couldn't really tell how bad the situation because of the poor lighting, but it was bad. If only you could have been at 90th replacement, seeing all the troops coming and going day and night. Our first morning there we were told, after we ate, we were to report to the staging area to get our orders. The staging area was a eighty by eighty square area, surrounded on three sides by barracks. The entire area was roped off in sections for the numerous companies. The other side of the staging area was open with a drive up area, where we were picked up behind the platform (ten by ten wide). The army personnel kept saying over and over for us to listen for our names to be called over the loud speaker.

A trooper who had just returned to 90th replacement from leave told us that if we didn't report when we were called, we would be sent to a high casualty area for not reporting on time. It didn't take a college degree to figure out that the company's with large replacement request meant that they were having a large number of casualties.

A couple of the Blacks stationed at 90th replacement warned us about the company's to be fearful of. We also learned when the Marines needed replacements the men who went first were the ones that didn't make the formations on time. When it was time to eat we also took turns watching our belongings while the rest of us ate. The troopers that stayed back sometimes didn't get a chance to eat all the time because sometimes even before we finished our meal our names were being called over the loud speakers.

We found out after the first formation that it was a no mercy rule when you missed a formation after one of the troopers that came over to Vietnam with us, missed a formation. I got back from lunch just in time to see the poor trooper leaving with some marines. It took about fourteen formations before anyone came for me and I got a chance to see almost all the Blacks leave who came to 90th replacement with me. Some of them went to high casualty areas unlike myself.

Chapter IV

After 90th replacement I went to Dau Tieng (A Battery) 1/27th artillery. I hadn't been in the company area ten minutes and I was already raising hell. When I walked up into the Orderly Room the first sergeant said, after making me wait for a few minutes, "What do you want boy?" Right away after my blood pressure rose fifty degrees, I told him, "I don't play that shit and my name ain't boy!" I had already made up my mind that I wasn't going to listen to that crap from anybody.

It wasn't hard to tell after that episode, that I had made a lot of enemies fast. The irony was that the rest of the Black's in the company felt that I was making things hard for them? This episode was my first taste of racism in Vietnam. Another unacceptable situation evolved in our company when I saw White soldiers being put in squads where they could make rank fast and the Blacks were put in squads where you might have to wait six to nine months to get any kind of rank. This was what was done to me.

After a few months I began to notice that the White soldiers who arrived the same time as me were being prepared to fill vacancies that were coming open within their squads along with being promoted. The vacancies in my squad had been filled just before I arrived in the company.

Before long it was promotion time. Three of the four White soldiers that had arrived the same time as me were promoted during our morning formation. Consequently, even before the formation was over I was raising hell about not being promoted. I couldn't really understand at first because I had learned a lot about the 155mm self propelled tracks. One thing led to another and I was on everyone's shit list.

Being Black in Vietnam

After I was left off the promotion list the second time around I began to try and figure out a way to get even. At first I couldn't figure out what I was going to do then the time came to give a donation to one of those Community Service Organizations was here. One Sunday during our afternoon formation they began to tell us about what good we could do for the people back home.

After the formation they brought around the slips for us to sign along with the amount the army brass wanted us to give. The first sergeant signed up about 60% of our company. Some of the soldiers were mad at the first sergeant because he told them how much that he wanted them to give according to rank.

A week later, a few more troopers had signed the donation slips and this time the captain spoke to the troops about giving. He told us that since our company had been in Vietnam we always had 100% participation. Then it dawned on me that I wasn't going to give, no matter what. After our next noon formation, there were still five holdouts and seven days to when the company had to have the sheets turned in.

The first sergeant appeased four of the five holdouts by offering them a three-day pass. However, I wasn't suppose to know anything about the pass. On the final Sunday the battalion commander came to our company formation to tell us that all the other companies had turned in their sheets and our sign up sheet was the only one left.

After the formation the first sergeant got desperate and offered to pay me the money out of his own pocket if I would only sign. I told him I wasn't going to sign until I was promoted. On the next to last day I had to go see the captain; he asked me why I wasn't going to sign? I told him if he promoted me I would sign and he said that he would give me some consideration the next time that it was promotion time. Then I told him, "I want my stripes now or I'm not going to sign." I went on to tell him, that due to the way I had been treated since I had been here in this company, I would consider it an honor to be the first one from the company that didn't give.

After a heated exchange between the captain and myself I was thrown out his office. I thought I had heard the last of the fair share routine but the very next day I had to go see the Battalion Commander. After I walked in and saluted the commander he started to talk to me and he never even asked me to have a seat. As a result of that treatment, I changed from a non-chalant mood into a nasty mood.

He fed me this bullshit about the tradition of the battalion and he couldn't understand why I was the only one in the battalion who hadn't given. I started by telling him that no one tells me what to do with my money and as bad as I had been treated around here the only way I would consider signing my name is that he would have to promote me.

The commander got mad and started hollering at me and I started hollering back and finally I just turned around and walked out the office. All the troops knew I was going to be on the shit list for not giving the money. As a matter of fact, the next morning by the time we had our work formation everyone knew what the company brass had planned for me.

The first sergeant was all smiles and he could hardly wait for the formation to end so he could give me my punishment. All the work details had been given out, and I was to go with him. Once the word was given for us to fall out, the first sergeant politely asked me to follow him.

Just about everyone in the formation was right behind us as we headed for the gate. As we walked pass the orderly room the first sergeant stopped to pick up a brand new entrenching tool (shovel) and he decided to carry the tool for me. We walked all the way out to the company boundary and then he stopped.

I was told that the rainy season was almost here and we needed a drain ditch dug all the way around the company area (around ten to fifteen acres in size) so the water could have somewhere to run off. The first sergeant was cheesing so bad that he could hardly finish his sentence.

The purpose of the detail was for me to refuse to do the detail but instead I said, "How deep and how wide." He said very angerly, "Two feet deep and two feet wide." Here we were right in the middle of an active war zone and I was asked to dig a drain ditch around the entire company area; not to mention the snipers lurking outside the gate.

I grabbed the tool away from the first sergeant and started digging. He watched me dig for around fifteen minutes with more than half the company standing there. By the time most of the troops had left the first sergeant was still there complaining about the way I was digging the trench. I had only three answers for all of his two thousand complaints. "OH YEAH, FOR REAAAALLL, and NO SHIT . . . ! I remember the last thing he said before he left, "I don't care how long it takes you as long as you get the trench dug!"

I continued to dig until he was out sight then I sat down and tried to figure out how was I going to get out of digging the ditch. I didn't have to figure out long because the minute I got relaxed along came the Vietnamese kids. The kids ranged in age from around seven to fourteen years of age. Their clothing looked from too small to too large in size along with being very dingy and faded. They were all very thin and it didn't look like someone had prepared them for school.

They saw me digging and walked over to where I was and asked me, "Why are you digging the trench way out here?" I told them I was on punishment and had to dig the ditch all the way around the company area. They thought for a second and then said, "We will dig for you if you give us the shovel?" I thought for a moment and it dawned on me that the entrenching tool belonged to the first sergeant. I agreed and those kids began to dig for me. While watching the kids dig I began to wonder how was I going to keep them digging for me all day?

I watched them dig for a while and along came our mess hall driver, driving out our company area; he was headed to the next post to pick up supplies for our mess hall in his five ton-truck. I flagged down the truck and asked the driver if he could give me a ride down to the village.

After we got off post, I asked the driver if he had anything to sell, while down here in the village? He laughed and said, "Yes." With his free hand he pointed towards the back of the truck where he had some half rotten eggs, withered vegetables, old meat and a few odds and ends.

I had the driver pull over where there were people standing around and I got out the truck and climbed into the rear of the truck and before I could finish looking over the merchandise, the Vietnamese people were trying to buy whatever I had to sell. I had sold everything within a matter of minutes.

Luckily for me that I got rid of the food quickly, because the MP's came along before the ration truck got out of sight. I had to hide because I couldn't be seen in the village, it was off limits, but troops still went down there.

I spent the remainder of the morning in the bar talking with one of the girls and drinking a few Vietnamese beers (A lot stronger than American beer). While down their in the village I paid the Vietnamese kids twenty dollars to watch out for the MP's and the VC.

I caught another ride back to my company before lunch and checked on the kids. I told the kids to be here when I got back and I would bring them something nice after lunch. When I left the kids, I soiled my clothes a little more and headed back to the mess hall. I must have counted the money ten times, as I walked back past the Orderly Room, headed towards the mess hall. While walking by, the first sergeant came out of the Orderly Room and wanted to know how I was doing, I told him that I already had done more than he could all day, and kept on walking.

When I first got to the mess hall, everyone kept saying, "You sure messed up this time!" I told the troops, "If this was the price I had to pay for deciding what I was going to do with my money, well so be it." I tried to look serious while I was talking to the troops, because I didn't want them to know that I was making money hand over fist, plus I had someone digging for me.

Before time for me to leave after lunch, I went and asked one of the cooks if he had anything for me to sell down in the village? He said, "Yes and bring me back some of the money." Most of the food I was given was perishable, except the coffee, sugar and k-rations. I said, "Okay" and I then left and went looking for a driver to bring the food down to the village for me.

I had the driver meet me outside the company area, so I could check on the kids and leave them some cigarettes. I repeated the before lunch routine and then when it was time for me to report for dinner, I once again threw dirt over my fatigues to make sure it looked like I had been digging all day. The kids had done a good job and I told them to return the next day and I would pay them again to dig. The drivers were waiting for me and I paid them off, and then headed for the mess bunker, where the cook lived, to pay him off. Everyone else in the company was waiting to see if I changed my mind about giving the money to charity!

It took a few days before the first sergeant finally caught on to what I was doing and he threw a fit but I got out of the detail. I had everyone laughing at the first sergeant because a lot of the troops thought it was wrong for me to be punished for not giving and they were glad to see me get over on the army brass. I might add the practice of selling food with the rations drivers continued without me.

Chapter V

After successfully staying within the guide lines of the army regulations with a little help from the troops, the company became desperate, they were ready to nail me anyway they could. One trooper who was friendly with me, overheard a conversation in the orderly room pertaining to me. He said, "The captain was beginning to worry about the moral in the company."

A lot of the soldiers didn't like what the company was trying to do to me because they were always trying to harass me. The Captain knew that if they couldn't control me, there might be other troops that would try the same things.

This one afternoon things were relatively quiet; we didn't even get called on once to fire a single round. Normally we almost always had at least three rounds to fire, if not our section, well one of the other five sections in our company.

Anyway the section chief was gone for the day. All week long I had been asking the section chief to go to the PX to do some shopping. He kept putting me off saying, "If things were quiet I could go." So the next day while the section chief was gone I asked the acting section chief if I could go to the PX? He said, "Its all right with me." Things had been quiet all that morning so I decided to go to the PX.

None of the sections had fired a shot all morning. However, as soon as I got to the PX, I could hear the sound of the 155mm guns roaring in the wind. I could hear at least three rounds go off. I wasn't really concerned because it wasn't our turn to fire anyway, so I figured that all I had to do was hurry a little in case there was another fire mission. Then it would be our turn to fire next.

Just as I came back walking up into the company area I heard another three rounds go off again (Boom, Boom, Boom). The section chief had returned and he wanted to know where I had been, so I told him, "It wasn't our turn to fire so I ran down to the PX."

The section chief went on to tell me, "I had to replace you and now the first sergeant is waiting to see you." I was really mad at what had happened. I began to question him about why he had turned me in to the first sergeant and he couldn't even look me straight in the eye with his under the shade tree answers. After a brief question and answer session I was on my way to the orderly room.

Before I could get half way over to the orderly room I had heard the whole story. One of the troops that didn't quite agree with how the army people were trying to deal with me, told me, "The fire mission was a fake." He said. "They were watching you when you left and gave you enough time to get to the PX." Then they called for a test fire. Since our squad wasn't up to fire next, they called for two three shot test fires instead of the usual three rounds. They even used two different squads including my squad.

As I approached the Orderly Room, the first sergeant was standing in the door with his arms folded. I could see a big smile on the first sergeant's face. It didn't take long however, for me to find out what he was standing there for. I thought to myself I wonder how fast that smile would disappear if he knew who my source was for the information about the fake test fire. As a matter of fact, normally when he saw me, he was mad at the world.

So with all 94 showing he said real politely, "Mr. Talbert, the captain is waiting to see you." I said, "Thank you Top" and I headed towards the captain's door. As usual I would make him tell me that I didn't knock and to go back out.

Ever since I heard that it aggravated them for me to do that I always made it a point to forget to knock. But this time the captain didn't say anything so to let him know how mad I was, I half-heartedly slammed the door shut. I walked over to his desk and asked what he wanted with me. He was so happy to have something on me that he let me get away without knocking or saluting.

He began by asking where had I been during the fire mission and I played dumb asking what fire mission? I didn't hear any shots being fired. He began assuring me that there was a fire mission and I countered by asking who done the firing and who did they fire at? The captain didn't know that I knew the whole story.

I had planned to stay there as long as possible and ask as many questions that I could get away with. I caught him off guard and he was really stumbling for answers. Finally he told me that I had violated company policy and I would be given an article 15 (admission of guilt, similar to a traffic ticket). If you don't sign you will be given a court martial.

So, I refused to sign and told him, "I wanted to see the Inspector General (IG)." The IG is a high ranking officer (colonel or above), who hears the soldiers side of the story and represent the soldier, along with making recommendations on the case. Also as in my case, listened to complaints from soldiers about other army personnel.

As I was leaving out of his office, I kept reminding him that I didn't hear rounds being fired and why was he lying to me about the rounds being fired? I tried to look as sincere as possible. I had already been told that the company didn't keep track of test firings. I had planned to wait until I saw the IG before I said anything about what I knew.

A couple of weeks passed and the Battalion Commander wanted to see me. He had to review any complaints before they were forwarded to the IG? The Battalion Commander wanted to know why I wanted to see the IG.

I told the Battalion Commander that I didn't hear any rounds being fired and the company was just picking on me because I refused to sign the charity papers. Finally after hearing all his bullshit, I was told that in order to cut down on all the confusion, if I would sign the Article 15 he would see to it that I would be given a light punishment, like being confined in the company premises for a couple of days.

I decided that if they didn't get me this time they would come up with something else. So I told him that I would sign and he sent me back to see the captain. Before I got back to see the captain, I saw my source and he told me that the Battalion Commander had called and gave the company hell for what they pulled.

Chapter VI

Right from the first day in Vietnam, I became introduced to the weird whistling noise. The first thing I learned was that the louder the whistle, the closer the rocket. The Vietnamese people were masters at firing those rockets. They could be walking down a trail and spot a target and blow it off the face of the earth. They also, would find our empty shell canisters and make rocket launchers out of them.

I remember the first day in Dau Tieng there was a rocket attack. The VC walked the rockets right across our post. The trail of destruction included a couple of bunkers, a vehicle and holes in the ground everywhere.

A couple of months later, I was close to where the Vietnamese workers were taking a break when we were hit with a barrage of rockets. One of the rockets hit about thirty feet from the orderly room. Right after the attack, one of the Vietnamese workers followed the rest of the troops over to where the rocket hit and when most of the troops left the Vietnamese worker walked straight over to the mess hall and then walked back over to where the other workers were. He saw me watching him and the next day a rocket landed about two feet from the mess hall.

When I walked over towards the mess hall to see what damage had been done, it suddenly dawned on me that the day before the Vietnamese worker was walking off how far the round landed away from the orderly room. I went looking for the worker but he was nowhere to be found.

I told the section chief and he said that he had also saw the workers doing the same thing several times before. The VC's favorite targets were the ammo dump, chopper pad and fire direction center. But they would settle for the mess hall, shit house or the other shit house (orderly room).

I had been in Dau Tieng about two weeks and a rocket hit the ammo dump and another one hit on the opposite side of the post, close to where the helicopters were kept. The third week I was there, the shit house was blown up and then another day the orderly room was hit. To my misfortune I didn't listen when the troops were telling me that when in the make shift shower, you wash as fast as you can and head for cover before you finish putting all your clothes on.

I got a chance to find out first hand what they were talking about the next day. There I was as usual, taking my time in the shower. Just as I was washing my hair, shampoo and all, I heard someone hollering, "In Coming." I almost tore the door off trying to get out of the shower. I had left everything, my shoes, clothing, towel and soap. My first step out of the shower let me know that I still had soap in my eyes, but that didn't keep me from heading for cover. A couple steps later, I heard the loud whistling noise and before I could react I had stumbled and fell. The fall was just in time because no sooner than I hit the ground, the rocket hit about twenty feet away. The force of the impact from the rocket, made the ground shake: just like it felt during an earthquake.

You can imagine how long it took for me to take a shower from then on. After the blast, I think it took me ten minutes to stop shaking and I never did finish the shower. I just got a bucket of water, rinsed off the soap and mud.

I remember another time when we were playing basketball and there were a lot of soldiers standing around watching us, then in came a barrage of rockets. Everyone was having a good time and all of a sudden we heard the whistling noise. In less than one half second the court was clear and everyone was running for the bunkers.

After the first rocket everyone was still trying to get to the bunkers and the next rocket hit not more than ten yards from where we had been standing. By the time the third rocket hit we were all inside the bunkers.

About a month and a half later, just as I was walking across the company area one of those giant rockets hit behind the orderly room and it made a hole about ten feet deep and twelve feet wide. You could tell that there wasn't a bunker in all of Vietnam that was thick enough to withstand a direct hit from a rocket like that. I was just glad that they didn't have a constant supply of those big rockets to shoot at us. Normally if no one was killed, we wouldn't fire back unless the VC kept on shooting at us from that location. Because the VC would fire a few rockets at us and then move their location before we could fire back.

Less than a half-mile from our base, the road divided the village from the rice patties, except for a few houses on the other side of the road. Located down the road from the village was this giant rubber plantation and the VC constantly launched rockets from inside the plantation.

We couldn't fire back at the VC when they fired at us from inside the plantation even if some of our troops were killed. Goodyear or some other tire company probably would have had our whole company sent to jail.

A major deterrent to the VC was the South Koreans. I had heard from one of the brothers while I was traveling that he was on a post in Quan Loi that had the Koreans camped on his post. At first the troops hated to have the Koreans on the post because a lot of the troops belongings kept coming up missing. About the third night of the Koreans being on the post, tempers were beginning to get out of hand and then they had a rocket attack on the post. A rocket landed right on top of the Koreans and killed a few of them. The Koreans unlike the Americans, gathered up their gear and left off the post in the middle of the night. On a normal walk you could be in the village in about fifty minutes, that is, barring any trouble.

Thirty-five minutes later, the Koreans walked into the village and killed everything living including all the animals. When they finally left out the village, all was left was a few iron objects that couldn't burn.

I was told that it sounded like an all out war, then all of a sudden the flames began to light up the whole area. The Koreans returned around an hour or so later and that was the end of the rockets hitting the post for a long time to come. Even the attitudes towards the Koreans changed.

Chapter VII

Right in the middle of all this flat land was this huge mountain Black Virgin (BV). You could see it from the ocean to the Cambodian border and it proved to be a menace to us. I had planned to do my best to keep from going anywhere near the mountain. The Army had a post right on the very top of the mountain. As a matter of fact, all they had including the small fire-base was a ten-acre plot surrounding the camp.

The armed forces caught hell all the time on the mountain. I believe the VC used the mountain post for training exercises and to practice war games on. There were ground attacks on that post almost as often as we had rocket attacks on our post. The Army didn't dare put anything of value up there because they knew that the VC were always willing to update their equipment. The helicopters that flew too low going up the side of the BV always seemed to draw fire.

The ideal time to fly up there was when the clouds hung half way down the mountain. The entire mountain was covered with trees, which made excellent cover for snipers. The middle of the BV was supposed to house a VC training center and a hospital. None of our soldiers wanted to go to the mountain because everyone knew about the large population of VC in and around the mountain.

I remember on this one occasion the army brass got this bright idea to try and take the BV. Our whole company was asked to go to the base of the mountain to support what looked like half the troops in Vietnam, along with the mechanized units. The first day we got close to the BV, the infantry and mechanized units were already close to the mountain base. We were asked to set up a small camp so we could support the troops and tracks that had been called in to take the mountain.

There was mass confusion the first day. The bulldozers arrived late and the barbed wire never came for us to set up a perimeter. The infantry troops set up listening posts about one hundred feet from where we had our tracks parked. All that first night we couldn't talk no louder than a whisper because we were interfering with the infantry, our conversations were being picked up on there listening monitors. We couldn't unpack our gear because we had to be ready to leave in a hurry in case we were attacked.

We already knew our position wasn't top secret because not more than a half hour after our arrival the Vietnamese kids came out of nowhere riding their bicycles with Styrofoam coolers tied to the handlebars. Inside the coolers were filled with ice and ice-cold cokes. The kids were selling ice-cold cokes for a dollar.

No one was suppose to know where we were going and along came these same kids we had left some forty or more miles back at our post. We had been riding all day and everyone was hot and bothered, and all we had to drink before the ice-cold cokes was water in our canteens.

The kids didn't have any trouble selling out and a few of the troops wouldn't drink any of the cokes because of the rumors we had heard about glass being put inside the bottles. Half the troops didn't care what was in the bottles as long as it was cold!

I was glad that the moon was full and there weren't any clouds because if I had tensed up any more waiting for daylight, I probably would have been as stiff as a three-week old corpse. We had to fill sand bags most the first day and part of the night. (picture) No one could sleep because of the air strikes on the mountain and the helicopters riding over us checking for troop movements in the area.

The second day the barbed wire came and we worked all day putting the fence around our position, making sandbag bunkers and getting ready for the assault on the mountain.

On the third day and a million sandbags later we were finally ready to support the taking of the mountain. Most of the makeshift bunkers had been completed and the place was beginning to take shape.

Early on the fourth day we got the word to stand by for the assault. The air strikes stopped and the infantry began to move up to the base of the BV. We had an estimated 100 tracks spread out going up the mountain with some of the troops riding or walking behind the tracks. A thick fog from the ships and airplanes pounding the mountain covered the base of the BV. We had already been told that we were staying until the infantry took the mountain. The troops had gotten about one third of the way up the BV and there were no VC in sight.

Then all of a sudden, all hell broke loose. The VC started to come out of their tunnels and they were on top of the troops so fast that all our troops had time to do was drop everything and run for their lives. Armed with automatic weapons, rocket propelled grenades and satchel charges; it didn't take long before the place sounded like World War Three. One of my home boys that was in on the assault said, "The only reason that a lot of his platoon made it back was because the VC were more interested in blowing up the tracks than killing them!" He also said, "The VC were firing volley after volley of rockets and mortars, and the charges seemed like it was raining down on their position, and the VC weren't afraid of their own shells. The VC didn't understand about taking cover, they just kept on coming."

Our company was less than a mile from the base of the BV and it sounded like the troops were firing every gun in Vietnam. I really felt sorry for the troops up there because all we could do was try and support them. It had been rumored that the assault had cost almost all the armored vehicles that had been taken up there. However, over the radio on our way back to Dau Tieng we heard that the assault on the mountain was successful and that the troops were holding there position half way up the mountain, they lost six tracks with 19 wounded and five killed. That was the last time I heard of anyone trying to take the mountain and away we went.

Chapter VIII

All the excitement seemed to fizzle down for a few weeks and we hadn't had a strenuous fire mission for a while. I also finally started to get used to carrying those 90 lb shells. My job was to go down inside the ammo bunker and get the shells, put fuses and powder inside the shell, replace the nose piece and carry the shell back to the track to be fired.

Normally we had rounds on hand to last a few hours, except for an emergency (long fire mission). We usually kept around one hundred rounds of 155m shells, powder, and fuses on hand. Then, before I could get used to sitting around we got a continuous fire mission that lasted about fifty hours.

The mission was really hectic and we had to work non-stop. After about ten hours of lifting and carrying those shells, my back began to hurt. We were already shorthanded and that meant that everyone in our squad had to help out because we didn't have enough people to make up a relief crew.

We were never really prepared for a long fire mission, either men or ammo. When the fire mission first started we were firing the rounds so fast that it was impossible for one person to get the shells ready to fire and bring them to the back of the track to be fired.

The bad part of the situation was that not one of the other three-crew members volunteered to double up their jobs to give me a hand getting the shells ready, and to take the shells to the track to be fired on time.

At first, I was trying to keep up but that didn't last long after seeing that I wasn't going to get any help. I realized after about twenty or so rounds that I wasn't going to get any help no matter how fast I worked.

The platoon sergeant seemed comfortable hanging out the window of the track, hollering for more rounds.

The first fifty or so rounds were easy to get to, but after that wave of rounds, the rest of the rounds were hard to get to. You could easily reach the first fifty rounds from the four-foot wide walkway down the center of the bunker.

The bunker had a six-foot wall lined with rounds, behind the opening when you first walked inside the ammo bunker. You had to walk down a five foot downward sloping floor about six feet long and one step on the end, before you reached the six foot wall of rounds stacked on top of each other and still in the crates.

The floor itself had a dirt base below the pallet lined four-foot wide space. By this time you are five feet underground and looking up at about an eight-foot roof that sloped down the father you walked inside. The roof was made of wood and steel beams and shingled with sandbags two foot high. Also the walls had sandbag siding about three or four bags deep.

Once inside the bunker there were two tunnels, one to the left and one to the right. On each side of the four foot walkway was lined with shells, fuses and powder. We used the two-foot by three-foot wooden pallets to help keep the shells from falling over. After about six more hours of continuous firing, we had to go to the ammo dump and resupply our shells, powder and fuses.

All that week the VC had been firing at the ammo dump and a couple of direct hits didn't blow the place up but the bombardment added to the holes that were already in the ground. The raining that had lasted for three days and no relief in site farther complicated the situation. So there we were in total darkness and on the road headed towards the ammo dump.

Our truck was equipped with night vision lights but you could hardly see anything with them, we had to depend on an occasional flash of light to keep us on the road. Most of the time, you couldn't tell if you ran off the road unless you ran into something that stopped you cold.

I had already made up my mind that the first sign of a whistle, I was going to head back to the company. There were a lot better places for me to be besides on the back of that army truck headed down the road with no lights. I didn't mind us running off the road every now and then but those misquotes were driving me crazy.

I kept hoping that we would go faster so I couldn't get bitten as often. After falling all over the truck for about thirty minutes we finally arrived at the ammo dump. The ammo dump was built similar to our ammo bunker except the walls were much higher and the dump didn't have a roof. The shells, fuses and powder were separated by double and triple stacked sand bags walls. A short ceiling covered the fuses and powder canisters from the weather. Plus the dump was large enough to turn two ten-ton trucks around in and a lot of room to spare. Several thousand rounds were stored there along with fuses and powder.

The ground of the dump, along with the holes was covered with about two inches of mud and a few inches of water. Trying to navigate through the ammo dump proved to be an almost impossible ordeal.

The monsoon (rainy season) saturated ground seemed to be impassible especially when you added in the giant holes filled with water and foot deep mud. Before we went twenty feet inside the dump we had to send someone back for one of the self-propelled tracks to pull us out of one of many craters.

We got stuck the first time trying to turn around and back the truck up to where the shells were stored. We got stuck the second, third and fourth times trying to get close enough to the rounds so we could just throw them on the back of the truck. We never made it that far because we decided to just bust open the pallets and carry the rounds one at a time back to where the truck was parked.

I believe that everyone for miles around could hear all the noise we were making, trying to get the tracks out the muddy holes. I knew then that our presence there wasn't any big secret.

When I first jumped off the vehicle inside the ammo dump, the mud stopped me cold. I almost fell over when I tried to take my first step. Both my boots were stuck and sinking.

Once I tried unsuccessfully to pull my boots out the mud before I finally had to take my foot out of the boot and pull the boot out the mud. As a matter of fact, if you didn't keep on moving the mud would suck you right down like quick sand.

We must have been at the dump for around two hours and I had fell down so many times while I was trying to carry those shells that they began to feel soft when I landed on one of them. Just as we were leaving the dump a rocket sailed overhead, landing about a hundred feet from our position. We were just about done so we turned on the truck lights and hauled ass out the dump.

Chapter IX

Once we got back to our squad area, I hurt my back while we were unloading the shells. Then after about thirty hours of constant sweating, all of a sudden I stopped sweating and became worried that I was dehydrated. I became sick and I laid down for a while and after not feeling any better I got up and started to work again. I kept asking myself when was this fire mission going to end?

All of a sudden I heard someone hollering outside the bunker, I thought they were hollering for more rounds as usual. However, just as usual I would ignore them and even slow down a little more. Too my surprise it was the section chief. He had crawled out the back of track after receiving orders from F.D.C. to end the fire mission.

When I looked up it was the Section chief, I thought he was standing in the makeshift doorway because I wasn't getting the rounds ready to fire fast enough, but he was there to tell me the fire mission was over. Then he said, "F.D.C. called and ended the mission." He also said, "As soon as daylight comes we have to go back to the ammo dump and clean up our mess we left." I was so tired I just lay down between the shells and fell asleep.

By the time I woke up, I could barely walk; my back was stiff and hurting. Once I struggled to get up, I could barely walk. I kept feeling like I didn't have my balance and I couldn't straighten up all the way at first.

Finally I made it out of the bunker and headed towards the mess hall. I was praying all the way that no one would holler out "In coming," because I knew if I hit the ground right then, I wouldn't get up again. That was just how bad my back was stiff and hurting.

Then the first chance I got I went to the doctor. During the first few visits the doctor waited on me without any problem and then I guess he got tired of seeing me and he turned on me. I guess he thought I was using up too much of his aspirin and muscle relaxers. Because on my next visit it was a different story and all hell broke loose.

I was the first one in his office and he waited on everyone except me and after everyone left he still hadn't called on me, so I just sat there. I knew that he had to do something because he couldn't just leave me in his office. So there I sat getting madder by the second.

Finally the doctor came out of his office and said real nasty like, "What do you want?" I snapped back, "What do you think I want, anyway why did you wait on everyone else before me?" He became real mad and said, "There isn't anything wrong with you."

Then I asked the doctor, "Why did you wait till now to tell me there wasn't anything wrong with me?" The heated exchange continued and I asked him to sign my slip so I could go and he started to walk away saying that he wasn't going to sign! When I jumped up and headed towards him, he changed his mind about signing the slip! The low life doctor also wrote in my file that I was just play acting and that I was just trying to get out of working.

That afternoon I went back to the orderly room to take my slip and complain about how I had been treated. I complained to the first sergeant about what had happened in the doctor's office. Although the first sergeant and myself didn't get along he knew I wasn't play-acting.

He told me to report the incident to battalion headquarters and I did. I was given the run around for three days before I finally got a chance to request the Inspector General (IG): advice from one of the army personnel.

The battalion commander didn't have any trouble calling the IG especially since the doctor wasn't under his command. When I went to see the IG he ordered me to go get some second opinions. I was given a list of doctors all over Vietnam and the IG told me I could choose which ever doctors I desired.

The first doctor I went to in Bien Hoa, I had to wait two days to see him and so I just hung loose and checked out the service clubs. When I was able to see the doctor the first thing he did was read my file and then gave me a two second exam and said, "I can't find anything wrong with you."

The second doctor I went to said the same thing and he also acted funny when he read the report. When I got back with the second report the first sergeant said that he hoped that all the reports weren't like that.

I waited a couple days and left again, this time when I got close to the hospital, I took all the derogatory parts out of the file. To my surprise, the doctor gave me a different report; as a matter of fact I stayed over a couple days while he ran some tests.

Altogether, I spent about a month traveling all over Vietnam while I was seeing all those doctors. While I was making all those trips I got a chance to meet a lot of Blacks from all over South Vietnam and was able to find out how they were being treated. Most of them said the same thing. They didn't have that much trouble with Whites who were equal in rank but it was a different story when we discussed the higher ups.

This one Black told me that when he first came to his company he was a supply clerk and that he had to go in the field for five months before he could get the clerks job and the soldier that they had doing the job wasn't even his classification.

A common occurrence was that there was a policy that after serving six to eight months in the field you could spent the rest of your time in the rear area. But when it came time for the Blacks to go to the rear area either the army was waiting on replacements or the Blacks were needed for important missions coming up.

Another major complaint was the lack of respect that they were shown. The army also seemed to try and keep us in the middle of the action as much as possible. On this one occasion I talked to this Black who had spent thirty days in Long Bin Jail (LBJ) as it was called. He told me that the Blacks outnumbered the whites ten to one.

Once when I was on one of these excursions, I met some Blacks who were on their way down to the village to see some women and have a good time and I went along. On the way back from the village as we were walking along the road these White soldiers came by and instead of offering us a ride they said, "nigger, nigger, nigger" and threw a bottle at us.

We were surprised at what had happened and about all we could do was give the soldiers the finger. The joke must have gotten good to them because they went down the road and stopped again and started hollering nigger, nigger, nigger again and we just kept walking towards them. To our surprise the soldiers started backing up towards us.

We let them heckle us until we got in range and then we rushed them. They tried to pull off but the jeep stalled and they jumped out and behind the jeep and then we fired some rounds at one another and before things got out of hand along came some more soldiers and they stopped to see what was going on, we told them and they gave us a ride back to the post.

The next day I saw one of the troops that had been shooting at us and he said that he was glad that no one got hurt. He also told me that those guys that he was with had been doing the heckling thing for a long time, and that he was glad that we handled the situation like we did. He said, "I don't blame you guys for what had happened and that those guys had been getting away with messing with Blacks for a long time."

By the time that I had finished my trips, I had as many reports that said I did have a bad back as I didn't have anything wrong with me. Once I turned my reports in, that was the last time I heard anything about the reports. The doctor had gotten transferred and that was the end of that situation. Army Justice.

Chapter X

Out of all the officers in the company there was only one that I did get along with and that was because I had a long talk with him about why I was acting the way I did. He understood but his hands were tied because I had made so many enemies. Most of the officers seemed to treat the Blacks okay but they seemed to fall short when it came to the things that mattered, like personal problems and rank. This one officer that I had a personality problem with really blew his cool one time during a volley ball game.

On the fourth of July 1969 the troops had a volley ball game against the officers and it started out as a pretty good game until tempers started to flair up. I remember I was playing on the net and no one seemed to be able to get a two-point lead. It was getting close to dark and there seemed to be no clear-cut winner. This one officer that I didn't get along with came up to the net playing across from me with the score tied. I got two jams in a row and the second jam hit the officer in the face when he tried to block my shot.

The shot didn't hit the officer that hard and all the troops let out a big victory roar. I even waited to see if he was all right before I joined in the celebration with the rest of the troops. The officer became furious when he saw that I was showing excitement. He responded by saying, "What are you laughing at I would have blocked the shot but all I could see is the color of your eyes."

I responded by telling him that if he would take off his shirt that I would give him something that he could see. Then when he didn't take off his shirt I began to call him down. I also told him that if he ever got disrespectful with me again I would kick his ass all over the company area and with his stripes showing.

The captain was out there during all the commotion and I told him that I wanted to file a complaint about what had happened. He told me to come and see him the next day and when I did he wouldn't see me.

After seeing how the captain had planned to handle the situation I got some statements from a few soldiers that witnessed the racist verbal attack. I also took the statements over to battalion headquarters and they kept me waiting for a couple days before I could see the Battalion Commander. He told me that he would have to wait for a few days for the report from the company before he could discuss the matter with me.

Finally after another few days of waiting, I was able to see the commander. He listened to what I had to say and then he said, "I will need to transfer you while the investigation was going on." That was the last I heard about the investigation and I was transferred to a different artillery battery in Tay Ninh. The captain sent along a nasty letter about me when I was transferred.

Chapter XI

At first when I arrived at Tay Ninh everyone had already heard about how much trouble I had caused and the first thing that I heard from my new squad was why do we half to take you? The first couple of weeks at my new home everyone was waiting for me to get into trouble and I defied all odds and things seemed to quite down after that. My new home B Battery wasn't as well kept as my first company but the atmosphere was a lot better. I really didn't see the clear-cut racial practices that were directed at the Blacks.

In Dau Tieng I was on a large base and we were more or less isolated from the Vietnamese people except for the ones that worked in the kitchen and around the base. However, in my new home we were constantly around the Vietnamese people.

I remember the first week at my new home I went down to the water hole where we obtained our water supply. If you can imagine a well right in middle of a cornfield, you can understand why our water looked like milk of magnesia. The water tasted like raw corn and I was forced to live on pop, milk and beer. I just couldn't bring myself to drink the water even after putting a purifying pill in the canteen.

Other than the water I went from hell to heaven. I didn't have any problems with the army brass. I must say I got along pretty well with everyone. After a few months there, the captain came up to me and said, "You will be getting promoted the next time the orders come back." I was really beginning to believe that there was going to be some justice to the system. As the few months came closer to an end so did my chances of making any rank. A few changes in personnel and again I found myself in the same situation as I was in Dau Tieng.

We had a new section chief and we were at odds right from the very first day. The new section chief hadn't been in the company five minutes and already he was trying to put me to work. He tried to make life miserable for me. He wasn't satisfied with anything that I did. When the rest of the troops were on guard duty the section chief wasn't anywhere to be found, but when I was on guard duty he was always coming around trying to find something for me to do.

Just about the time he was getting a kick out of trying to harass me, I got my chance to get even. We had to get the entire company cleaned up because a high-ranking officer was supposed to be coming to visit our base. Orders had come down from battalion for the place to be spotless and the order included cleaning everything even the ammo bunker and the 155mm self-propelled tracks.

The section chief made his own day when he thought about all the nasty jobs that he could have me doing. Consistent with the way he had been treating me; there I was again with all the menial jobs. The section chief and his buddies got all the technical cleaning jobs inside the track and whenever the section chief looked my way, he was all smiles.

His crew kept busy cleaning everything that they could get apart on the inside of the track. My job was to clean everything on the outside. Whenever I needed some help on the outside the whole crew would come out to get enough done to where they thought I could finish by myself.

A classic case was when we had to clean the muzzle and firing tube on the self propelled tracks. The troops also needed my help, plus everyone else they could find when it came time to clean the muzzle and flash tube. The muzzle had to be screwed off the flash tube, and it really proved to be an ordeal, especially if the muzzle hadn't been off in a long time.

The task was accomplished by putting a metal pole through the openings in the side of the muzzle and with everyone's help, you could barely break the muzzle lose from the flash tube. The flash tube was cleaned like you clean a chimney on a house. The rest of the crew helped me until one person could run the cleaning rod up into the tube by himself. I even got a chance to clean up the mess the crew made on the inside the track.

I was really mad over the way I was done and all the time I was working, I kept saying to myself, I know I'm going to get even some kind of way! Time was growing short for us to have the place cleaned up and the first sergeant was beginning to get nervous. Everyone was busy running around trying to get last minute chores done.

The first sergeant inspected our living quarters, self-propelled track, company area and munitions storage area. He praised the section chief on what a good job he had done with the area, and our area was cleaned the best in the company. Even the track was spotless inside and out.

No sooner than the first sergeant left, the section chief told everyone to take a break and then he looked over at me and said, "I noticed that there were some fuses and powder that were out of place and for you to go straighten them out."

I told him that I was taking a break like everyone else and besides the first sergeant had said that our area was the best in the company. He asked me if I was refusing and I told him, "What do you think?"

He ran all the way over to the orderly room to report me for not obeying him. I didn't care because I knew he was just messing with me. Before the section chief could finish drueling all over himself we got the call for a fire mission.

As usual, I was given the call to get the shells ready to fire. We were kept on standby for about four hours. While we were on standby was when the crew first noticed that they couldn't get the breechblock in the track to close all the way. The breechblock is the mechanism on the end of a cannon that must be closed before you can fire a round, something similar to the hammer on a pistol.

When finally the order came down to fire, the section chief reported that we couldn't fire because we couldn't get the breechblock to close. Another squad was given the order to fire. Same outcome, they couldn't get the breechblock to close.

Finally after calling all around the company, no one could fire a round. The high-ranking officer had just arrived and was shocked to find out that none of the sections could fire a round. The high-ranking officer cancelled his departure and said that he wasn't leaving until the matter was resolved. The company resembled hells night, there were a million answers to the problem but no solutions.

The company had done such a good job cleaning the tracks that they couldn't even get one of the breechblocks to close. The VC fired some rockets at us as usual and we couldn't return the fire even though we knew where the rockets came from. After a few hours of the monkey trying to bang the football, the high-ranking officer directed the company to call in Ordinance (which is in charge of the maintenance of the tracks) with no results.

On the second day the main Ordinance from Saigon was suppose to report to our company after there were no results. I was on guard duty and once I finished duty I decided to take a look in the track and see if I could figure out what was wrong. The VC got wind of the fact that we weren't able to fire back and you could go down on the bunker line and almost see where the rockets were coming from. I guess the Gross National Expenditures for our government must have rose a few points because of all the gas the helicopters used riding shotgun around our camp trying to keep the enemy from overtaking us.

The morning I came off guard duty all night, I was on my way back from duty when I decided to go into the track and see if I could straighten out what was wrong. After assessing the situation for a few minutes and trying to get the breechblock to close, I began to feel comfortable about what I was looking at.

It only took me a couple of minutes before I noticed that the breechblock was in the wrong position to close (Something I remembered from training class in Fort Sill, Oklahoma). I can still remember the instructor telling us that the block won't snap shut if you don't cock the firing mechanism!!

During the excitement that followed I was on my way to get the section chief when I noticed he was on his way to the club to wine down. Then it dawned on me that this was my chance to get even. Once inside the bunker I told the acting section chief that I thought that I could fix the track. He looked up from what he was doing for a second, then without saying anything he went back to what he was doing. I left the bunker in time to see the section chief disappear out of sight. Next, along came the high ranking officer walking across our company area heading for the orderly room with all the ranking officers in the company. Making sure that everyone heard what I said, I saluted the Brass and told them that I knew what was wrong with the firing mechanism.

At first the captain tried to dismiss me like I was a kook and the high ranking officer said, "Can you fix the damn breechblocks" and I said, "Yes sir I can." I must have been the only E3 in history to be leading around one of the highest ranking officers in Vietnam. I was leading the high ranking officer over to the track and he was asking me why I hadn't said anything before now. I told him that I had just figured out what was wrong and that no one would probably listen to me anyway.

One of the troops was already inside the track when we arrived. I had him help me pull the breechblock back apart and this time we turned the handle until the spring depressed, putting tension on the spring. Then when we attempted to close the block again, the firing mechanism snapped into position. What we done different was, we turned the handle back across the spring until the spring was depressed and the lever moved into position. I remember that part of the booklet from training camp showing the firing pin in that position.

Once we loaded the chamber we called for permission to test fire. That was the quickest 10-4 that we ever had gotten from F.D.C. Usually you had enough time to get the coordinates, fuse the round and load the shell before you were given the ok to fire.

During my chance at fame, the acting section chief came inside the track and was trying to claim that what I was doing wasn't going to fix the problem. Some of the troops didn't even bother to plug their ears because they didn't believe the round was going to fire either. By that time F.D.C. had called back and said, "Fire the damn thing." To prove his point the acting section non-chantilly pulled the cord and the old pile of junk unleashed a thunderous roar that could be heard from miles around.

The acting section tried to act like he was alright, but when the cannon recoiled, and grazed him, I knew that he was hurt because he looked like he was going to pass out. That was the first 155mm round to fire off our post in three days. Everyone came running over to our track to find out what we had done to fix the breechblock. What really made my day was that the section chief was just getting back to our squad area when the smoke was clearing from the round being fired.

The section chief had left his drink at the club and came running back over to the company area to find out what had happened. While on his way he saw the first sergeant and asked him what happened. The first sergeant told him that while he was down at the club setting on his dead ass Talbert fixed the breechblock.

The section chief was in total shock bordering traumatic immobility, especially when he saw the captain coming out the track. The first sergeant had followed the platoon sergeant over to our track and watched him trying to walk normally, but everyone knew he had just come from the club!

After all the brass had left our area the section chief wanted to know how did I fix the firing mechanism. He was told that I waited until he had left the area and went and told the captain that he knew how to fix the breechblock.

The section chief was really mad at me and he walked around fuming for a whole week because I really made him look bad. He consoled himself a little when he found out that I had to see the first sergeant. That brought back a few smiles on his face.

A couple of days later I was called over to see the captain. The section chief was grinning from ear to ear because he knew that if you had to see the captain that meant that you were going to get punished.

However, if you had to see the first sergeant that meant you was in big trouble.

I walked over to the orderly room and the first sergeant said, "The captain is waiting for you." Sure enough when I walked into the captain's office, he had the article 15 already typed, lying on his desk, right in front of him. The captain told me what the report from the section chief said and he asked me if I had anything to say.

I began telling him about how the section chief had been treating me and about how he refused to listen to me the morning he left for the club. I had tried to tell the section chief that I thought I could fix the track and he responded, "So What!" He then said, "I don't give a damn what you can do I'm headed for the club." I also told him that the section chief told everyone to take a break after the cleaning was done except me. Then the section chief told me to go to work and I didn't think that was right. That was the reason I refused!

The captain didn't say a word after I finished and just started to tear up the article 15. The captain also told me how important it was for him to maintain order and everything. The next thing I knew, he told me to report back to my section. I saluted the captain and said thank you sir and away I went.

On my way out of the orderly room the first sergeant stopped me and asked what had happened to me. I told him that I was just supposed to report back to my section. He looked surprised and nodded his head and just about that time the captain came out his office carrying the torn up article 15. I watched the captain take the wad of paper and drop it into the trash basket.

The captain then told the first sergeant that he was headed for his bunker! I watched the door close behind the captain and then when I looked around at the first sergeant, he looked like he was lost for words. I then said, "See you later Top" and left.

On my way out the orderly room, the large smile I was wearing grew larger and I ran all the way back to the section with a giant grin still occupying my face. However, before I could cover the entire distance, back to our squad area, some of the troops met me part of the way and wanted to know what happened to me? I told them that the captain was thinking about making me section chief. During the commotion the section chief was peeping out from behinds the sandbags of our bunker. As loud as we were, you could hear us all over the company area.

It didn't take the troops long to change the subject from me becoming section chief to what about the article 15. After this sequence, one of the troops turned and hollered back to the bunker housing the section chief. "Hey Sarge, the captain just made Talbert section chief." The section chief couldn't take it any longer and left our bunker with the afterburners going full blast, headed towards the orderly room.

He met the first sergeant coming out the orderly room and asked him what happened to me. The first sergeant told him that the captain tore it up. The section chief didn't bother me any more after that; I think he was afraid of crying wolf.

After the incident with the section chief things began on the upswing again. My biggest asset was that I never tried to gloat and myself along with the section chief began to get along. The captain even had a talk with me about getting promoted in a few weeks. I started to count the days before the three weeks were up.

About a week before promotions time I was on duty and a shell fell breaking my toe. The small firebase I was on didn't have a large hospital and I had to go to a larger base for treatment (Chu Chi). Once a cast was placed on my leg I was ready to go back to my unit. The doctor asked me where I was stationed and I told him I was at a small firebase out in the field. He said I couldn't perform any duty that required me to be on my feet.

The first few days I was back in the field no one bothered me about doing any duty, because I was still on crutches. The situation changed quickly the very minute I stopped using both crutches. The first time we were shorthanded the section chief wanted me to perform guard duty so I had to do the guard duty for one night in the middle of monsoon (rainy season).

My cast became wet on more than one occasion and started to dry rot and come apart in the next two weeks. I guess that by being a racist the section chief just couldn't stand seeing me setting around doing nothing.

A few weeks later when I returned to the doctor, I told him that the company had me on guard duty on more than one occasion. I also told the doctor that the racist section chief couldn't stand seeing me sitting around doing nothing. The doctor looked at what was left of my cast and got mad and put on my slip that I couldn't return to duty until my foot got well, so I had to stay at Battalion headquarters where the hospital was.

When I returned to my company area to get my belongings someone told the mess sergeant that I couldn't eat in the mess hall any longer because I was transferred to our company headquarters. I was also told I couldn't get promoted because I was going back to Battalion headquarters??? I thanked the captain for thinking about me and I left the rest of the company in the field.

Chapter XII

At first, headquarters acted like they didn't have anywhere for me to sleep, then they gave me a bunk as far away from the mess hall as possible. I was surprised at how I was treated but I didn't let the treatment get in my way.

The first couple of weeks in the rear area were getting hectic for me because of the crutch, I had trouble getting around and I had to depend on the Vietnamese kids, who worked in the mess hall to run my errands for me. The trips to the mess hall everyday really wore me out.

Then when I went to the orderly room to get my pay, I was told that they had sent the money out to the field and I would half to go out there to get it. I was mad and broke but that didn't last long. One of the soldiers who was suppose to pick up the Vietnamese house girls every morning had to leave the post for a few days and he asked me to pick up the workers.

The first morning on my way out to the gate, I saw the kids and they told me that if I wanted to make some money all I had to do was let them pick up some call girls. They also told me that all I had to do was step outside the gate and they would round up the call girls. Since, I could only pick up a certain number of workers, I made sure the sergeants, whom all had private house girls done without them for a couple days.

All the regular house girls were already at the gate to be picked up, so I told them that the sergeants had to leave for a couple of days and they could return when the sergeants got back. True to their word the kids rounded up the call girls and once the regulars saw who was replacing them I had to step back inside the gate to insure my well being. The regulars were cussing me and screaming at the call girls and kids.

The first morning of our planned operation, I had two problems, one was I had to keep the girls away from the sergeants, because I already had to explain to the sergeants why their house girls weren't there and I surely didn't want the sergeants to see the call girls in the company area. The second problem was where were the girls going to operate? I solved both problems at the same time when I had the girls operate out of my bunker. (Picture)

The other troops who lived in the bunker were gone all day. I told the girls that if anyone asked what they were doing here, tell them that they came in with the company across the street. Once the sergeants came to find out where were their house girls, I just told them that the girls weren't out there at the gate! I already knew that the sergeants wouldn't take another girl until they found out what happened to their regular house girls. Luckily for me the sergeants came to my bunker before the girls got started. The troops were trying to bargain for a group rate, seeing how payday had passed.

I stood outside guarding my bunker while the girls were getting ready to operate inside. Once the girls settled in, I went over to the nearest club and told a few troops that I had some call girls and there was a stampede over to my bunker. However, I became worried when I saw the line getting long, going into my bunker. I didn't want to have a problem with the sergeants who saw the troops coming over to my bunker. I told most of the troops to go back to the club to wait until someone came from my bunker, because we didn't want to get caught and the girls couldn't come back anymore.

A while later after lunch, I made the girls knock off early because they had to clean my bunker up before they left for the day. When the girls were ready to leave, I was paid off and everyone was happy. To my surprise no one told any of the sergeants what was happening so we ran the operation smoothly all that day.

That evening, a few of the sergeants whom didn't have a house girl found out about the operation and the first thing that they wanted to know was why didn't anyone tell them where the call girls were? I just told them that I would personally bring them one of these girls if they wanted one.

On the second day, the regular house girls were determined to get inside the gate and when I stepped up to the gate, the house girls were arguing with the call girls and the kids. I started to try and get the attention of the kids without stepping out the gate. The gate guard saw what I was doing and told me, "I had to go outside the gate to get the workers!"

By that time the kids saw me and when I stepped outside the gate, I made sure that if the guard needed a light, I wasn't out of range to give it to him! When the kids started walking over to where I was, the call girls and house girls were right behind them and still arguing over who was going inside the gate. The kids had to protect me from the house girls.

Normally, the girls stood in different areas outside the gate so the different companies wouldn't have to go out and round the workers up. There was always a large crowd out there looking for work. Most of the time if one of the regulars didn't show up, the rest of the regulars would have a replacement picked out for whoever came to pick them up.

One of the sergeants whose house girl hadn't missed a day in six months wanted some answers as to why his house girl had missed two days in a row. I told him that she wasn't out there and if he didn't believe me he could come out to the gate and see for himself. However, no one was willing to come out to the gate because it was dangerous sometimes.

Later that afternoon, when it was time for the call girls to go, one of them was missing. I became worried until I found out that the missing girl was at another bunker doing her thing. Finally, I got the girls back to the gate and my money making venture ended because the next day the regular soldier returned. The practice continued after the second day because the troops were really glad to see the girls and one of the sergeants gave up his house girl for the cause.

I also instructed the kids to comb the countryside and bring me back some really good smoke. After turning down a couple of samples the kids finally showed up with a winner. The weed was grown with opium plants and instead of the texture being green the texture was a real dark green almost black.

The troops gave the smoke the title "black power" because all you needed to do was to be close to someone who was smoking a joint and you could get extremely high. The smoke became so popular that everyone on the post was always looking for me. My favorite clients were the troops coming out of the field for stand down. They would give their right arm for a joint. The smoke was so powerful that you could smoke on a joint for almost a whole week!

After the women, drugs and the booze, the poker games became an all day affair. There were always enough people around to play poker. The favorite target was the troops coming out the field to go on leave, they always had plenty of money! Sometimes the troops who played cards with us had to borrow money so they could go on leave.

I remember this one time a trooper who didn't play cards at first, watched his two friends that were going on leave lose all their money and some of his. Finally he decided to play for himself. He wore us out and won all his money back, his friend's money and a lot of ours.

Chapter XIII

It was getting pretty close to Christmas time and I wanted my foot to heal so I could go to Saigon for Christmas. A few trips to the doctor later and I was on a walking cast. You wouldn't believe the number of times the company personnel went to see the doctor trying to get me back in the field. The doctor at the hospital kept reminding them that I was still under his care and I was staying where I was at.

For the next few weeks, I began to get around more and more. I kept doing the exercises, day in and day out, trying to help my foot to heal faster, and I did fairly well. Once my cast came off, I was fitted with a smaller cast, and again the army personnel were right back to see the doctor, trying to get me back in the field. The Captain also told the mess sergeant not let me send the Vietnamese workers to pick up my meals anymore.

The company brass didn't know it but, I also was able to sneak down to the village to pick up a few supplies for myself. I didn't have anything to worry about whenever I left the post because the kids looked out for me, I was their meal ticket.

This was a basic agreement where I always looked out for the kids and they returned the favor. I remember when I was catching all those helicopter rides to go see the different doctors I would tell the kids where I was going and before I could see the doctors the kids would have followed me to the destination.

Some of the kids had followed me from Dau Tieng to Tay Ninh. I could go down to the village and the kids would already have checked out the village to make sure it was safe for me. I always gave them money and all kinds of food and other goodies.

60

When after a few days on the walking cast, a letter came from the bank address to my company commander. The letter stated that my savings account was overdrawn and they wanted immediate repayment.

What happened was when I got ready to go on leave, I went to the bank to draw out some money to trade with some troops that had just came back from leave. I withdrew the same money again once I got to Hong Kong on leave after my money had run out. I went to the bank there and my account was still in good shape. The withdrawl hadn't shown up yet so I was able to draw out the money again. I was going to repay the money when I returned.

What I was looking for was someone who I could get to change army money for American money. Money the troops had left over from leave that I could trade with them instead of them taking that money back to the bank.

You couldn't spend American money out in the field but you could trade the army money in when you went on leave or going home. This was a common practice, seeing how you were only allowed to carry so much money on leave, according to your rank.

Another more common practice was, you ask someone from home to send you some cash in an envelope and you take that money and trade for at least three times as much in-country money and then send a money order back to the source.

I was summoned to see the captain and he confronted me about the letter from the bank. I told the captain that I wasn't sure if I owed the bank the money or not, because I had lost my copy of the bank statement. He agreed to let me go to Saigon to see about the letter.

After leaving the orderly room, I headed to my bunker and grabbed all my cash and camera and headed for Saigon. I left the kids in Tay Ninh because I was going to Saigon to party.

The first day there I went sightseeing and took a few pictures, while passing the bank numerous times, and finally I waited until about five minutes before closing and walked in and asked for the persons name on the letter. The bank personnel told me that I would have to come back the next day and away I went. It didn't take long to find a bar and pick up a girl and I headed for the hotel for the night.

The second day, I returned to the bank to find out about the letter and they didn't have a copy of the bank record at that location to show me, so I told them to send the statement to my company and if it showed that I owed some money, I would repay it. The bank people agreed to send a copy of the record to my company, and I asked them to give me a letter stating what we agreed upon and they did.

Once outside the bank, I looked at the date on the letter and it said the 13th and I changed it to the 18th, and away I went. I only lasted a couple of days and I was almost out of money. I only had enough money to either do some sightseeing and buy a few drinks or pay for a room and a meal. I choose to sightsee and hang out at the bars. This was a three or four day vacation because you are not in a hurry to return to the field.

My first few stops, troops were buying me drinks and my money was still in good shape until later in the day. My last stop I was pretty well loaded and I was sitting in the bar with a girl and before I knew it, darkness was beginning to set in. I suddenly realized that I didn't have enough money to pay for a room before curfew. I started begging the girl with me to let me stay with her because I didn't have enough money to pay for a room.

At first she was hesitant because she didn't think that I was going to pay her back for letting me stay with her. I figured that this wasn't the first time she had heard this story. There I was, stuck in the club with the bartender telling me that I had to go. The girl didn't agree to let me stay with her until the bartender started to turn out the lights.

Just as we were getting up to leave, in walked Ed and at first I didn't recognize him with his hat on. He didn't have any trouble recognizing me though. I had my hat in my hand. Before I could take a step Ed said, "Hey Donald, man what are you doing in here? It's curfew time." I told him that my company had let me come down here to take care of some business at the bank. I also told him that I had ran out of money and I had just got the girl to agree to let me stay with her for the night.

Immediately Ed reached in his pocket and pulled out a huge wad of bills and pealed off a few and gave them to the girl and told her that I was going with him. By this time the bartender had all but one light turned off and Ed told me to come on and go with him. I thanked the girl while we headed for the door.

On our way to the door we began talking about how surprised we were to run into each other. Back in Flint growing up we only lived less than a block from each other. Once outside you could see the darkness had begun to set in but people were still walking around like it was still daylight.

Ed said, "Follow me" and we headed for his cycle and driver, which were less than ten feet away. Ed said he was going to show me around Saigon before we went to his apartment. I asked if he wasn't worried about being out after curfew and he said, "After curfew is when everything is happening here."

When we reached the cycle Ed told me to get in and he walked around to the driver and told him that he wanted to ride around for a while and the driver nodded. Ed walked back around to the other side and got in and we took off. We barely had room to sit because of all the artillery that was already taking up room. There were handguns, rifles a grenade launcher and all sorts of munitions. Ed said, "I have gotten used to being out after curfew while he continued to show me all his artillery he carried in the cycle."

I asked Ed if he knew the driver and he said, "I pay him so much money that everyday he is parked outside of my apartment or if I'm at work he is outside the gate waiting for me." He makes sure that I don't ever need another driver for anything and he always makes sure nothing happens to me. I guess I was a little afraid because I didn't know what to expect.

The streets were filled with smoke from open fires as people were cooking out in front of buildings. There were men and women walking down the streets with guns strapped over their shoulders. Men and women sitting or squatting out in front of the buildings acting as if the war was going on back home instead of right here.

This sure did beat being back in the company, where we didn't know if we would make it through the night or not. Even some of the kids were out playing. In the background you could see the light flashes from bombs going off all over the countryside. What really surprised me was there were as many people out at night as there was in the daytime. The only thing missing was the army personnel. I didn't see any at first, but not long after we left the club, we were making a right turn and inside this old car was a brother driving and I told Ed and he said, "You haven't seen anything yet."

As we approached more and more cars and trucks, some American made, I kept trying to see if there were any brothers driving or riding. A little while later, Ed had the driver stop and Ed asked me if I knew any of those brothers that were walking. I couldn't believe my eyes, because one of the brothers walking, I had been in basic training with. We stopped and talked for a while, and he had been living down here for a few months.

He was living with this Vietnamese lady and had a baby on the way. He told me that he had been living off the black market and asked me for my ration card. I gave it to him and we had a long talk about living in Vietnam and he told me that he had planned to stay over there forever. I told him what I had thought about staying over there and Ed agreed with me! I just couldn't give up seeing my family and friends again, plus I had a job waiting for me back home.

I remember we left there and rode around a while and then we passed Long Bin Jail (LBJ) and the place looked like a real dump. All you could see was barbed wire, sand bags and those large towers. Around the entrance, there were Vietnamese troops with tents in the background. The place was well lit up with the guard shacks in the towers hanging over the walls. That was one place that I didn't want anything to do with.

Another place I remember visiting was Soul Alley. There were at least twenty Blacks living down there and they were all absent With Out Leave (AWOL). Most of them had Vietnamese families and the whole works.

When we first pulled up I didn't see any brothers; even when Ed had the driver pull over and stop. Then it seemed like they were everywhere. We got out of the cycle and stretched for a while. I asked Ed if this was his grand showcase for the night and he said, "The big surprise was later on." Then we walked inside this building and I saw this brother and a Vietnamese girl sitting at a table. I looked at Ed and he wasn't surprised at all. He said, "There is a lot of Blacks staying down here in the alley."

We stayed there for quite a while, took some pictures and finally Ed said, "Let's go" and we walked back outside climbed into the cycle and the driver drove off. I noticed that each time we stopped the driver wouldn't go with us, but instead he would hop off the cycle and go talk with some of the Vietnamese people in the area. I remember as we headed down this one street I couldn't help wonder what else was in store for me, really I thought I had seen it all!

After a brief trip up and down a few of the major roads, we drove up in front of this building and we got out. Ed said, "This is part of the surprise" and we walked past the guards out in front of the building and one of the guards spoke to Ed as we were let inside the building. We walked down the hallway to the stair weld and walked up to the third floor.

There I was in disbelief as Ed opened the door to his apartment and turned on the lights. The place was filled with all sorts of luxuries that I hadn't seen since I left the states. We were surrounded by everything except a cash register and showcase. Sarcastically, I asked Ed where were they? He smiled and said, "As fast as this stuff leaves here, we don't need a showcase and as for a cash register, we couldn't find one big enough to hold all the money that goes through here, plus I only have one customer."

He told me to pick out whatever I wanted and I could take it with me! I told him that I didn't have anywhere to keep the goodies and that when I was ready to leave country, I would come back down and take him up on the offer.

Before I could walk around and check all the goodies, in walked Ed's contact and he gave Ed a whole bag of money and he introduced me to his contact. While they were talking I glanced around at the T.V's stereo equipment, watches, rings, kitchen appliances you name it. Almost everything you could find when you go shopping. Ed told me that the goodies belonged to him and a few more people.

Once we left the building, Ed's driver made it to the cycle about the same time as we did and Ed told him to take us home. When we climbed into the cycle and on our way Ed told me that the rest of the surprise was coming up later after we made another stop.

A short time later, Ed told me to take a look on the left and I saw these Military Police (MP's) guarding this hotel with people coming and going just like in the daytime. Ed said, "This is where my army bunk is and the MP's stay here also!" The place looked like a fortress as we rode by. I kept waiting for the driver to pull up and stop but we just kept on riding.

We rode for a while and drove up in front of another hotel building and Ed told me to take a look on the left. This time there were Vietnamese Army guards outside standing in front of the place. Behind them there was barbed wire about six feet high all around the building. Behind the six to eight feet of wire there was a large wall, all around the place. As we were getting out the cycle I asked Ed, "What's going on here?" He said, "This is the other part of the surprise."

We walked past the guards into the building. Once we got inside, Ed began to tell me about some of the people that were living there. They were mostly civilians living there and a few army personnel, those that could afford the rent. The inside of the building looked like a modern day hotel, the walls were even painted! As we walked down the hall and up the steps, Ed kept asking me, "Have you figured out the surprise yet?" I told him, "No" and he started laughing.

Once inside we walked up to the second floor where Ed's apartment was. Down the hall on the same side was the other part of the surprise. We walked up to the other apartment first and Ed unlocked the door. Once Ed opened the door and turned on the lights, the place looked like the warehouse all over again. He had this place filled with some more luxuries. There were even goodies (clocks, watches, clothing, jewelry, TV sets and all that helped fill the place) in the bedroom.

Once he showed me around there, we headed for his apartment. The apartment looked like something out of a magazine. I mean he really had the place laid out. The best music equipment money could buy. Camera's, diamond watches the whole works. After we left his living room, he showed me the two bedrooms and bathroom. That was the first time I had seen any hot water or a tub since I had left the states, I thought I was in dreamland.

He had all the latest sounds from the states on a reel to reel along with albums and tapes. He was really living like a king. Through out all the excitement, I had forgotten to tell Ed that I was hungry. Before I could ask him if he had anything to eat, he asked me if I was hungry and I told him yes.

He got up walked to the door and said, "I'm going down the hall to get my woman." I sat there on his couch and listened to some sounds until he came back with his woman. She cooked steak and potatoes, a salad and we feasted. While I was still eating, Ed got up and went into the bedroom and made room for me in the middle of all his possessions.

After we ate, I took a bath and just as I was coming out the bathroom when I knew anything Ed had the girl that I had at the club and she was standing in the doorway next to him with a big smile on here face. Ed had told his driver when we were leaving the club to bring her later on. Once the few shocked seconds passed I said, "Man how did you find her again?" Ed just said, "Money talks."

Chapter XV

We staid up most of the night, drinking booze and talking about back home. The next morning after the Vietnamese girls had left; I went to work with Ed at the post office. It was really a large operation. The post office was even handling merchandise for the Vietnamese stores.

After seeing all those guards, I couldn't help but wonder how the troops were getting all the merchandise out the place, especially those large items. I thought to myself, "They must have some tunnels dug underneath the place."

While inside the Post Office we walked around and greeted some of the troops that worked down there. After Ed would introduce someone he would tell me if they were stealing or not as we were walking away. As it turned out almost everyone that he introduced me to was stealing even some of the officers.

After all the introductions I walked with Ed to where he worked next to the damaged package cage. All he had to do was rewrap the damaged packages and some sorting. I asked Ed if I was suppose be in there while he was working and he replied its okay because this wasn't his shift, but he had to work later that night.

The packaging room was separated from the much larger room by a steel cage and steel door. Ed saw me staring down at the floor and I would bang the floor a couple of times. He asked what I was doing and I told him, "I was looking for the trap door and tunnel that they used to get the goodies out."

Ed laughed and said, "We don't have to go through all that trouble." He showed me around some more and then he asked me if I wanted to go for a ride and I said, "Okay."

We walked outside the building to where they kept the delivery trucks and Ed told me, "Get into the second truck" we walked up to the truck and I climbed in. Then Ed climbed into the driver's seat and we drove to the gate past the security station. The MP's waved at us as we rode out the gate (Mom and Pop type security)!

After we got outside the gate and drove down the road Ed told me to look in the back of the truck and Ed said, "This how we get the goodies out the place." We drove to the warehouse and Ed had the guards unload some of the merchandise off the truck and we left. Then we drove to Ed's apartment.

Once there Ed asked one of the Vietnamese guards to help him unload the rest of the merchandise off the truck and take the merchandise to his other apartment. When we got ready to leave I told Ed that I wanted to take some pictures and we picked up my camera at his apartment and headed back to the Post Office.

I wanted to take some pictures of Soul Alley and we swung back by there on the way back to the Post Office. On our way back we went to find Ed's contact and he gave Ed a bag full of money. I was dropped off at the same club I was at when Ed found me and Ed said he would be back later to pick me up.

About an hour later Ed showed back up and we spent the rest of the day hanging out before we went back to the Post Office at almost curfew time. Ed had to report for work. Once there Ed said, "They had another fake bombing" at the Post Office and that he was suppose to be assessing the damage with some of the workers, which probably was going to take up most of his shift.

Ed walked me back to the gate and motioned his driver and asked him to take me back to his apartment. When we got there he found Ed's girlfriend and she took me up to Ed's apartment and went and found the same girl I had the night before.

Chapter XVI

My fourth day in Saigon, we were out riding around a couple hours before curfew and Ed took me over to his girlfriend's mother's place. He wanted to give his girlfriend some money and have her take care of a few things for him.

When the driver pulled up in front of the building where his girlfriend's mother lived, I never imagined what I was in for. When we first walked into the building there was a long hallway with rooms on both sides. None of the rooms had door handles or locks, I guess that was what made me nervous and tense.

The feeling intensified when people kept opening the doors in front of us and behind us as we walked along the hallways. The intensity grew even greater after trying to look down the dim lit hallways to see where we were going. Without ever stopping to inspect the lights, they looked like candles inside a jar. The halls were filthy with dirty unpainted walls and a low ceiling, no decorations. The floor was a different story however, I couldn't tell if the floor was all dirt or just filthy.

I noticed that Ed was walking faster than I was because I was just walking and looking around. I also noticed that Ed was about to walk off and leave me so I hollered and said, "Slow down, are you headed for a fire or something?" He just laughed and said, "You will see." So I rushed and caught up with him.

When we reached the end of the hall there were two halls leading in opposite directions. We took the one on the left and it was another long hallway and it also had rooms on both sides.

At the end of this hallway to the left was a set of steps. We walked down the hall and took the steps to the third floor and when we got there, their was another long hallway with rooms on both sides and at the end of this hallway was another and another. We must have walked up and down these hallways at least ten times. Finally, Ed said, "We're almost there."

Then we went up a couple short flights of steps and down the hall a few doors. I asked Ed if there was another way out and he said, "This is it." We didn't have to worry about knocking because by the time we got close to the door; the door came open and we never had to break stride walking into the room.

As we cleared the door, I noticed the one big room was sectioned off and the room looked like the halls and floors we had just left. Inside the room I couldn't help but notice the absence of a kitchen or restroom, there was only a table and some chairs and a few spots to sleep on, along the wall.

Now I understood why so many people were cooking outside! Ed's girlfriends mother was standing close to the table and Ed gave her money and told her to give the money to her daughter for her to run the errands for him.

While inside I had an urge for a cigarette and as I was reaching for my jacket pocket, I thought if I light up in here and a fire starts, I never would make it out alive. So my hand just fell limply away from my pocket and the urge to smoke went on. The same thought (fires) also answered the earlier observation of people cooking outside.

We were only in there a few minutes and Ed was ready to leave. Once we got out of the hotel I took a good look at the place and decided that it was the largest structure that I had ever been in during my entire life.

Actually the place really didn't look that big when I looked and saw that it was only a few stories high, but so were the rest of the buildings around there. I would hate to have had a job as a deliveryman! In my world when you needed more space you build up not out.

Ed was looking for the driver as soon as we walked outside the building. The driver was talking with some other Vietnamese people and when he saw us, we all made it to the cycle about the same time. I was glad I left my camera in the cycle because I was already ringing wet from the walking and I needed to have my hands free at all times while walking thru them hallways.

It was time for Ed to go to work and we headed for the Post Office. While on our way back to the Post Office I took some more pictures and did a lot of looking around. It was unreal seeing all those army vehicles riding down the streets.

Once at the Post Office we went in past the security through a lot of rooms and walked back to where Ed worked in a different area than before when he showed me around. Ed knew everyone and we didn't have any problem getting back to where Ed worked. Once there, he started looking at the packages and also handling them.

About ten minutes after he started to work a friend of his came into the caged area and pointed to a package that was on the sorting table. Ed said, "Ok" and he pulled the package off the table, away from the rest of the packages. The camera's were inside cardboard and wrapping paper including a company label saying, Nikon L.T.D.

The two of them immediately opened the box and inside were two brand new cameras. Ed said to me "This camera looks just like yours." After they finished taking all the wrappings off, Ed's friend took his camera and left. Ed said, "I'm going to take some pictures with you when I get off." I gave him some of my film (while he was taking the tags off the camera) I had inside my film pouches. Ed laid the camera down next to mine until time to get off work.

Late that night we were ready to leave and I asked Ed if he was going to take the camera out the gate with him and he said, "Yes." Without looking back at Ed, I just picked up my camera and started to head out the place with Ed walking behind me.

On our way out the gate we had about fifty feet to walk before we arrived at the guard booth. After we walked about thirty feet the new

MP's saw us coming and right away they moved their position so that they were blocking the gate. I knew right then that they were going to stop us. Sure enough when we got within ten feet from where the MP's were standing they started walking toward us.

The one MP said, "How are you doing and where are you guys heading?" The other MP said, "Those are some nice looking camera's you guys are carrying." By this time they were both looking at the cameras. One of them commented that the camera's sure look new. I told them that I bought my camera about a month or so ago. The MP's looked at each other and the one closest to me said, "May I see your camera" I said, "yes and be careful how you handle the merchandise because I got film in it." The MP took my camera and checked to see if it had any film in it.

My camera had film in it and then the MP's saw the film pouches that were looped over the camera case strap. I even had film inside most of the pouches. I glanced back and saw Ed trying to hold back his smile.

The one MP looked at the other MP and said to us, "Okay" and they stepped aside and we walked on out the gate. Our expressions changed from a slight smerk to a large grin by the time we had crossed the street. We walked about twenty feet and Ed's driver pulled up and away we went. We thought we had heard the last of camera incident but as it turned out we didn't. Ed had his driver stop at the first bar and we untensed ourselves.

Chapter XVII

As we were walking out the bar, I noticed these soldiers coming out this pharmacy down the street from where we were. I asked Ed what were they buying in the pharmacy and Ed said, "Lets go see."

We crossed the street and walked over to the pharmacy and went inside. The Vietnamese man behind the counter motioned to us to come over where he was and he showed us this bottle. I will never forget the label. The bottle had a picture on the front of a really obese man (like Pluto standing next to Popeye) standing next to a man that was about the size of a featherweight. The label read, Obesotol. The Vietnamese man behind the counter remarked "Last one."

I looked at Ed and said, "I don't have a prescription?" Ed laughed and said, as he was reached into his pocket for his wad of bills, "This is the only prescription you need!" I looked surprised including disbelief before I saw the Vietnamese man reach for the money with one hand, palm up and passed Ed the bottle with the other hand, palm down. Then the Vietnamese worker smiled and said, "Number one." I guess Ed didn't react fast enough for the Vietnamese worker because after a short moments pause he looked at me and said, "Last one."

Then another soldier that walked in behind us and came up close enough to overhear the worker talking and he said, "Damn I came all the way down here for nothing." Ed said to the soldier, "Go ahead brother, you can have it. We just wanted to see what everyone was buying."

The soldier said, "This sure is some good stuff." It will keep you woke and high indefinitely. I usually drink it when I'm on bunker guard duty. Ed looked at me and said, "I don't have bunker guard" and I said, "Me either." We laughed as Ed and I walked out the store.

On our way back to the cycle, I told Ed that it was time for me to go back to my company. I also told him that the date on my slip had almost run out. Ed laughed and said that he thought that I had planned to stay down here for good. Then Ed said, "First we're heading back to my apartment and you can leave from there."

Once we got back to Ed's building we stopped by Ed's storage apartment and he offered to mail me home a few goodies and give me some money, I only took the bag of money. I was given so much money that I couldn't fit all the money into my front fatigue jacket pockets.

On my way to catch a helicopter ride back to my post I ran into the Vietnamese kids whom had came all the way down to Saigon looking for me. I decided to go back with the kids including riding the Vietnamese buses. During our trip back we went on a buying spree all way back to my base. Every store we stopped at I would ask the kids to pick out what they wanted and I would buy whatever for each one of them.

When we finally got back I gave the Vietnamese kids all the Vietnamese money I had along with some of the army money. I didn't want to take all that money back to the company with me because some of my pockets were still bulging with money. I also didn't want any more money than I could keep my eye on!

Chapter XVIII

For the next couple of weeks after returning, I was having a ball with my new found wealth. I was glad I had gone to the doctor and told him that I was taking a few steps without my cast. In only a few days I began to feel comfortable without the cast and I had just started to run a little.

Then in the next few days, I was walking down the basketball court dribbling the ball at first and later running on the foot. Once my cast officially came off for good, I started to play basketball everyday. It didn't take long before someone from my company saw me playing and told on me.

The company brass went straight to the doctor and told him what I was doing and the doctor still wouldn't send me back to the field. The doctor was overheard telling my first sergeant that I wasn't even suppose to be in a combat zone with a broken foot. The sergeant became mad and went and told the mess sergeant not to let me eat in the mess hall anymore! I didn't care because either I would go to another mess hall or I would get some food from the mess hall and have the Vietnamese workers cook for me.

Again when it was payday, I was told to go out to the field to get paid instead of the rear area like the rest of the troops who worked in the rear area did. However, I had already countered by going to the P.X. a few days before payday and getting as many troops as I had money for to buy cigarettes, soap and candy for me to sell.

From the mess hall, I would get whatever I could and I would tell the Vietnamese kids I would be bringing the stuff to them. They in turn would be waiting for the rations driver and me to get the goodies for them to sell. We could also trade for whatever else the kids could come up with.

Just to make it look like I was hurting for cash I would complain vigorously to the first sergeant and captain about having to go to the field to get my pay. The company brass didn't know it, but I would head out to the field with all sorts of goodies to sell. The first sergeant would always say, you're still assigned to the field and that's where you will be paid, not here! Then he would go back to doing whatever he was doing before I interrupted him.

Chapter XIX

Things were going along smoothly for me until the Army Intelligence (AI) came to get me. The company brass thought that they were rid of me, but AI told my company that I was wanted for questioning. I didn't know what was going on.

As far as I could figure, I could only be a witness. AI told the first sergeant that my next home was going to be L.B.J.! Then they put the handcuffs on me and I was taken away.

We traveled half way across Vietnam and I was handcuffed most of the way. Traveling by helicopter, we had to make about six stops. On the next to last stop I got into an argument when one of the guards said something I didn't like, we got into a shouting match within a matter of seconds.

We had just arrived at the heliport and were waiting in the makeshift depot. The place was almost empty and all I asked the guard to do was take off the handcuffs, so I could get a drink, he got smart with me and I got smart right back with him. We got into a heated exchange and all of a sudden, a whole bunch of infantry troops (mostly Black) walked into the depot and right away, they saw that we were arguing and they walked right over to where we were.

The guard saw all those brothers heading over our way and instantly he got quiet as a church mouse. All of a sudden the guard decided to take the handcuffs off and let me go get a drink. When I saw the fear in his eyes, I got even louder!

He reached in his pocket, pulling out his keys in a hurry; trying to reach for my hands I just pushed him away! By that time the brothers were over there on top of us. When they saw the handcuffs, they asked me what was going on and I told them, that I was just wanted for questioning and the guard didn't want me to go and get a drink! The guard told the brothers that I was wanted for questioning by AI (big deal). The troops weren't about to leave us until I told them that I had things under control.

However, I made the guard sweat for a while before I told the brothers I had things under control. The guard was scared to death, all them brothers had just come out the field, they had been out chasing tax collectors for the last four days. The brothers were out hiking through rice patties, which were seemingly on every square mile in the country, mined roads, villages and tall grass, sometimes with very little rest!

The VC would appear out of thin air and go into a village and take what they wanted and leave. By the time the army would be called in and get on their trail, the VC would already have moved on to another village. But, before leaving they would leave a few sniper behinds to hold off the troops.

The typical feeling amongst the troops was they didn't mind the walking; they however, didn't care too much about being harassed by snipers. The guards were really glad when it was time for us to leave. They didn't bother me any more the rest of the way!

Chapter XX

After traveling for another hour we finally arrived at the AI headquarters and right away AI started playing mind games with me. At first they acted like they were taking me straight to LBJ. Next, I was taken into this room and quizzed about the two camera's. I told them that the only camera I knew anything about was the one that I had and it belonged to me, and I had proof. They kept telling me that if I didn't cooperate I was going straight to LBJ!

For the next couple of hours they fingerprinted me and all the time they kept reminding me about LBJ. They also took about ten pictures of me. Once AI finished taking the pictures they decided to take me outside for everyone to watch them take more pictures. I really got mad when they kept me outside taking pictures for about a half hour. AI was really having a ball however, they didn't know it but they had just killed any chance of me cooperating with them.

Once we got back inside their office, AI started to question me again. Then they asked me to make a statement about what happened in Saigon. I told AI that I went to work with Ed and after staying there his entire shift, Ed and I left. I went on to tell them that on our way out the MP's stopped me and asked about my camera. I showed my camera to them and the MP's said okay and we left.

AI wanted to know about the camera Ed carried out. I told them that I didn't notice the camera Ed was carrying until we were stopped at the gate. They showed me a statement Ed had made: I read the statement and it didn't say anything about the money or goodies Ed had given me or anything else about the large operation going on at the post office.

Being Black in Vietnam

After listening to the bullshit for the rest of the day I was told to go back to my company and produce my receipt for the camera. I had the receipt in my pocket but I didn't tell them that. I was asked to make a statement about what had happened and I refused to tell them that I knew the camera Ed had was stolen in spite of the fact that they knew better.

I was asked why was I down in Saigon and I told them that I had to go see the people at the bank. They asked me why was I at the post office and I told them that Ed was showing me where he worked and afterwards, how to get back to the bank when he got off work. I gave AI the name of the bank.

Once I was released I wasn't given any travel orders to go back to my post so I was on my own to get back the best way I could. I had to hitchhike most of the way and was lucky enough to catch a couple rides on helicopters the rest of the way.

When I returned to my post I was confined to the company area until the company heard from AI. My company didn't like the way AI was handling my case because they were promised a replacement for me and it never happened. Also the Brass grew tired of me playing spin the bottle with the Vietnamese workers!

AI had my company's attention although, until they told the company about me being suspected of being the ringleader of this huge black market operation. Everyone in the company knew that AI was full of shit if they had me pegged as the ringleader of that black market operation.

My company was even asked to keep me confined to my bunker until they heard from AI again. The company brass was all smiles because they thought I was going to LBJ BUT NOT FOR BEING THE RINGLEADER OF THE SMUGGLING OPERATION, because they knew better!! The captain could have stepped up and said that they had the wrong guy but he didn't?

However, to help matters out the company told AI that I had been involved in numerous black market schemes along with selling drugs

82   Donald Talbert

and call girls. The company even said that I frequently took trips and always came back with large sums of money.

A couple of weeks later AI sent for me again and this time my section chief was told to bring me. The company was furious when they found out AI was taking both the section chief and myself away from our duties, because they needed replacements.

When the section chief and myself showed up in Saigon I was again questioned about my camera and about being the ringleader of the operation. I just told them that if they didn't believe me they could ask the section chief who brought me down here.

They brought the section chief in for questioning and he confirmed my story. He told them that the camera I was carrying belonged to me. He also told AI that he was right there when I sent off for the camera and that I had been on duty everyday except for when I had to go see the doctors and then I had excuses. AI was almost in tears by the time the section chief finished his statement.

When they brought me back in for questioning again they began to question me about the warehouse. They knew about it and wanted me to show them where it was at, along with who the contact was. Ed admitted to AI that he had told me about the operation. AI wasted no time waving all the statements in front of my face.

After I finished reading the statements, saying I was the ringleader of their operation, I was told that the troopers had all been court martial. The troops made it sound like I was their contact and that I would meet them in front of their hotel and pay them off. I told AI once again that the only time I had been down in Saigon was when I went to the bank!

AI was determined not to let me go back to my company until I told them that I would help them catch the Vietnamese cab drivers involved, who I was suppose to be selling the goods to. I was told by AI that if I showed them where the warehouse was and helped bring down the operation I could get off lite with maybe not serving any time. What a grand gesture!

Before the section chief and I left Saigon, I dropped my section chief off at the bar and I went to find Ed and he was under house arrest. I told him what had happened and he said that if I told them where the warehouse was, he would be facing jail time. Ed also told me that he had lost his rank and was going home as soon as the investigation ended, which was on the same day that I was suppose to be going home.

The section chief and I returned from Saigon and that was the end of the investigation, as far as I knew. By the time we got back to the post everyone knew that I was facing big trouble and the company helped set me up. The section chief had told everyone in the company that AI thought that I was the ringleader of a large black market operation.

The section chief also told a couple of troops that the company was helping to set me up for a big fall. You should have seen the first sergeant listening to his chance to get rid of me going up in smoke!

A few weeks had passed and I had a week to go before it was time for me to go back to Saigon and set up the sting with AI. AI had instructed my company not to give me my orders to go home because they would take care of them when I came back down there.

Two days before I was to go back to Saigon, I spent the remainder of my days clearing post and getting all my belongings together. With two days to go, I was sitting in my bunker and decided to go over to the orderly room and find out how was I suppose to get to Saigon.

On my way there I met a soldier in the company who I had never said two words to, all the time I was in the company and as a matter of fact, I was about to walk by him without speaking when he stopped me. He said, "I hear you are suppose to be going home but you won't be getting all your orders to get there."

My first inclination was to tell him to shut the hell up but instead I just said, "Yeah." He went inside his shirt and pulled out the missing parts of my orders to go home. I asked him how did he get the rest of my orders and he just said take them and don't ask any questions!

Then the day had arrived for me to go back down to Saigon and AI had requested that I was to be escorted back down to Saigon and the company decided that they weren't going to send anyone with me because they were already shorthanded and they didn't want to see me anymore.

I was given my orders to go home and told that the rest of my orders to go home would be sent separately and handled by AI. I left the post with all my belongings and headed for Saigon.

Once I got there I went to find Ed and he was still under house arrest. Ed told me that he had a lot of loose ends to tie up and he couldn't go anywhere. Ed also told me that he was leaving country the next day and he needed me to go to the apartment and get his belongings and some odds and ends that he wanted; because everywhere he goes the guard goes.

First I had to check in at AI and tell them when I had planned to set up the sting. I told AI that I had to get everything lined up and I would be back in a couple of days. Once I left AI headquarters I went back to Ed's barracks.

I had left all my belongings at Ed's barracks and found his cycle driver across the street from where he was confined. I asked Ed's driver to take me to Ed's apartment. When I arrived his girlfriend was there and I didn't tell her that Ed was fixing to leave country the next day. I told her that one of the other post offices had been blown up and Ed had to go there to fill in for a couple of weeks. She asked me if I wanted her to find me a girl for the night and I told her no; because I was tired and just wanted to rest. She said okay and left.

Ed's girlfriend left and I packed all his belongings and laid down for a while. Ed had told me that his driver was his girlfriend's brother. The next morning I was up before the crack of dawn and left the hotel to find another cycle large enough to carry all the baggage. I had to make two trips into the hotel to get everything Ed wanted.

However, I left the apartment with less than half the things Ed wanted me to get because I just couldn't bring anymore and I wanted to get out of the apartment before his regular cycle driver showed up. I had to squeeze into the other cycle and I asked the driver to drive me around until daylight, and then take me to the airport.

When we arrived at the airport, I had the driver get me as close as possible to the customs staging area. I had to wait there several hours before Ed and his escort showed up with all my belongings. Ed was really happy when he saw how much of his belongings that I had brought along.

We were escorted to process out at the air terminal. When the guard gave the processing clerk Ed's orders, my orders were also given. Then the guard said to Ed, "This is where I'm supposed to leave you," and he left.

Once the guard left, Ed said, "I thought sure you would go AWOL instead of showing up here? You came down here like you were daring anyone to mess with you." I told Ed, "The only thing off the table was me volunteering to walk into an (ambush), I mean sting operation."

The clerk at the terminal looked at my orders and asked if I also was leaving country and I said yes. He took the copy of my orders and went to another office and returned about a half hour later and said, "Ok the flight is leaving in about four and a half hours."

I also needed to get paid for the last two months and another clerk came back shortly after and walked me to another window to get paid. We still had at least three and a half hours before time for us to leave Vietnam.

We asked one to the troopers we knew to watch our belongings while we made a run to buy a few items to take home with us. He agreed and we left the air terminal. We caught a ride on a cycle and went to downtown Saigon and bought some luggage. We brought two matching sets and Ed needed some extra suitcases for all his belongings. When we finished all our errands we got back about a half hour early and put our belongings into the suitcases.

Just before we left to board the plane we walked around until we found someone from Michigan and gave him all the Army money that we had left and a few more things. We told him that we were going to give him a good start and to enjoy himself. He was really glad and thanked us.

Shortly there after, we boarded the plane and I was looking out the window and saw the MP's heading towards the plane. I really became nervous but I didn't let on that I was expecting the MP's to be coming to get me. Then, Ed asked if I thought the MP's were coming for me and I said, "I hope not."

Just as the jeep got closer to the plane, I subconsciously began looking for my belongings I had put in the overhead. I just knew the MP's were coming for me! The jeep stopped at the boarding platform and I closed my eyes.

The next thing I knew Ed was asking me if I knew the brother whom they had escorted here? He was another 212 discharge ruined for life by the army. I breathed a sigh of relief after the MP's left and the loading ramp pulled away. When the plane finally landed in Guam, the plane couldn't leave fast enough for me.

Once we arrived in Hawaii the Army authorities were asked to surrender me to go back to Saigon and the authorities in Hawaii said, "We need authorization from Oakland." After another long ride (Eight hours) we arrived in Oakland and it was too late to send me back because I had already changed duty stations.

After the plane finally came to a squelching halt, no sooner than the steps were in place, we were inside the plane maneuvering for position to be the first one to get off the plane. No one seemed to pay any attention to the stewardess when they were trying to tell us to stay seated until it was our turn to exit.

When we stepped out the plane in Oakland the customs were all set to welcome us home, especially me. Once inside the terminal the customs welcomed us home. Our luggage was unloaded and then customs walked us over to these long rows of tables. The customs inspector told everyone that if they had anything that they weren't suppose to have, well this is their last chance to get rid of it.

We were told, "We are going through everything you have and if we find anything at all, well this is as close to home as you will get!" The inspector continued, "Now I want everyone here to place your belongings on both sides of these last three tables, and open your suitcases. Take out anything that you aren't supposed to have and leave it here on this first set of tables and nothing will be said. Now if we find any contraband you're facing ten years at hard labor.

The custom inspector went on to say, "We are going to be calling you by alphabetical order and when you hear you name called, raise your hand so we can identify who you are."

The inspectors started off just like they said they would and after about the first ten searches a few more troops would walk over and drop off some contraband on the first table. After they saw a few more troops get weak in the knees the inspectors speeded up the searches. Instead of inspecting every article the inspectors would glance over most of the belongings.

Unfortunately for the inspectors some of us already knew how the inspectors were going to search. We had already talked to some of the troops that came home on leave and they told us that if you are one of the last ones in line you could bring just about anything home.

When the inspectors got to the T's they passed right over me. I walked over and told the custom inspector that they had passed over me. He asked what was my name and I told him and he said, "Bring your belongings and come with me."

I was surprised at the answer and I asked him why did I half to go with him? I really got scared because I thought I was on my way back to Vietnam. The inspector said, "There is a hold on you from Vietnam."

I was asked to follow him into this room and that's when he asked me what happened over in Vietnam and I told him nothing. Here I was in this small room and it didn't take long before the customs inspector started to check everything I had in my possession.

The inspector went on to say that I was going back to Vietnam for questioning as soon as they could get my orders signed. Then, before the inspector finished checking the first suitcase, I was told that I had to go see the post commander so he could sign my orders to go back to Vietnam.

After about an hour wait I was finally escorted in to see the post commander. When I walked in the room he was already reading my information. He left me standing there for about ten minutes while he continued to read my information. I was really feeling low when the commander asked me, "What the hell did you get yourself into over in Vietnam?"

I told him that I didn't do anything wrong and they were just trying to make me the fall guy for this large smuggling operation, they had at the post office. He asked me what did I know about the operation and I told him. I said, "Almost everyone at the post office was in on the scheme and I believe some civilians working for the Pacific Architect and Engineers, were also in on the operation." I continued that some of the troops would serve their duty and stay in Vietnam working for that company.

Then he told me that, "I'm not going to send you back to Vietnam because whatever they think you did, well they should have taken care of the matter over there." He went on to say, "What's missing here is a statement from you admitting guilt or any sign of a court martial to make this report believable." As he was signing my orders to go home he said, "Farther more you have changed duty stations."

Then the commander finally looked at me and said, "Where do you live here in the states and I told him in Flint, Michigan. He went on to ask me some more questions about the large operation. Then he told me that I had made the Central Intelligence Agency's most wanted list and in the same breath, he called the clerk in the office and told him, "Get this man a ride to the airport because he has missed too many flights home already."

The customs inspector who was waiting in the next room came in and couldn't think of anything else to say said, "He hasn't been through customs yet." The commander didn't even answer him and said "That will be all!" I went back to the airport, picked up my bags including an ivory carved statue of a Vietnamese woman and a child, an ivory carved chess set and a Rolex watch. I was given a ride to the train station while the custom inspector was watching me all the way out the door. If asked I would have gladly paid the duty charges, but I just figured the army owed me that much.

When my leave was over I had to report back for my last four months of duty. Once I reported back to Fort Sill, Oklahoma I found out that I had been reported as AWOL. (Picture) I was only there about two hours an again the Vietnamese issue came up and again I was put under house arrest.

My record took about eight days to make its way back to my new company. Again I was questioned about what happened in Vietnam. I gave the same answer "Nothing." The captain decided that the report didn't make any sense and he said the same thing as the commander in Oakland "That anything that should have been done to me should have been done over there."

The captain was really amazed that with all the charges I had against me, and my name being on the most wanted list, why wasn't anything done over there in Vietnam? My answer was that, "I am only a private." The captain laughed and said, "I am also amused by your company report, especially after reading the part of the report showing about you being on duty every day for almost the entire time I was over there."

He also asked me, "Why was I in Vietnam a whole year and never given any rank?" The captain continued, while he took a look at my almost clean record and said, I'm going to promote you and that he wanted me to work at the service club.

I took advantage of my great job and I also was a sports reporter for our army paper. I also won the Army-Air force chess tournament and place second in the ping-pong shoot out.

In looking back over what happened in Vietnam I can only conclude it was a disaster for many soldiers of color. Economically speaking the most benefit that we got out of the war for the rubber plantations was a chance to say that we served for our country in spite of the fact that we were called baby killers back home.

We were left out of the money making end of the deal. We didn't own any of the company's that made war materials and we were lucky to even get jobs working for these same companies. The only benefit that I could see from us going to the army was the training and schooling we received. We can't match this accomplishment in our own communities, right here in this country. The school systems constantly educates us without us learning to read or write good enough to get any type of satisfactory employment.

It took affirmative action for us to even be considered for most good jobs and the rest of the jobs, seemed to be unattainable. The least thing that these companies could have done was see to it that us troops were treated fairly. The anger continues when I think about how some Black wounded soldiers like myself were done and I didn't even get a purple heart.

Ammo Banker where I worked out of

Ice Cold Cokes

Ice Cold Cokes

Black Virgin Mountain, Due Bow Den

Soul Alley, Saigon

Soul Alley, Saigon

Prostitute in my bunker

Assault on Black Virgin Mountain.

Trash Run

Preparing for assault on Mountain.

Edwards Brothers Malloy
Thorofare, NJ USA
March 11, 2014